GREEN WILLOWS

GREEN WILLOWS

Jan Alexander

CHIVERS
THORNDIKE

This Large Print edition is published by BBC Audiobooks Ltd, Bath, England and by Thorndike Press, Waterville, Maine, USA.

Published in 2004 in the U.K. by arrangement with the Author.

Published in 2004 in the U.S. by arrangement with Wieser & Elwell, Inc.

U.K. Hardcover ISBN 0–7540–9918–0 (Chivers Large Print)
U.S. Softcover   ISBN 0–7862–6279–6 (General)

The text of this Large Print edition is unabridged.
Other aspects of the book may vary from the original edition.

Set in 16 pt. New Times Roman.

Printed in Great Britain on acid-free paper.

British Library Cataloguing in Publication Data available

Library of Congress Control Number: 2003115688

PROLOGUE

I have come at dusk, come to follow the little path that leads over the hill and down by the lake. It is no idle curiosity that has brought me back to Green Willows, nor any longing to see the place again. For ten years, I have lived down the road, and in all that time, I have never set foot on this path. Hardly anyone ever does. Hardly anyone ever did.

But I have come because I must, come because someone saw, or said he saw, two ladies down by the lake, and I must know. I must see for myself.

He did not come with me. I told him where and why I was going, and he looked at me with a look I thought to see no more in his eyes. After a long while, he nodded and turned away from me. When I left, I looked back once, and he was in the doorway watching me. If I had asked, I am sure he would have come, but I did not ask, and he did not offer.

So I have come alone over the hill, around the stand of birches. The path is overgrown now; the wildness had always threatened, and now it reigns triumphant. Brambles catch at my skirt like warning fingers that would hold me back when I press on.

And there is the lake, with the willows that gave the house its name gracing one green

1

bank. It is a pond really, with an island in its center and a gazebo on the island. It is artificial, of course, dug out when the house was built, but it is deep. Deep enough for drowning.

The little gazebo is crumbling now, and its roof has fallen in. The little stone bench that once sat there is turned over, its legs stuck into the air like some great clumsy animal that has been rolled on its back and cannot right itself again.

I come closer, my gaze going beyond the lake. There stood the house on a gentle rise, and beyond that, the cliff and the sea. What a contrast that was, to walk from the front to the back of the house, from this lovely, peaceful view that was artificial, to the real waves crashing at the real rocks below. There was a clue there, in that duality of nature, if I had been clever enough to see it at the time.

But I do not walk to the cliffs, which I never liked, or to the house. There is no house there now, only two broken chimneys that stand like sentinels watching me approach the lake.

There are no ladies by the lake. There are no ghosts here; they were long since driven out.

And yet . . . and yet, why do I turn my head so fast, thinking for a second that I saw a girl racing across the hill, flinging herself to her death over the cliffs?

I catch my breath and sink into the tall, soft

grass by the water's edge. I close my eyes, and at once, memories beset me. I see the gazebo clean and lovely, gleaming white in the moonlight, and I see a man standing in its shadows. I see a young woman moving quickly through the darkness, across the bridge (the bridge, where is the bridge, is it gone too?), and into his arms.

I see another scene, too, less romantic. I see two women struggling together by the water; I see them fall into the water . . .

The wind rustles the branches of the willows, and it is the sound of gentle sobbing in the night.

Someone screams.

I open my eyes and sit up, my heart pounding. But it was only the cry of some bird, a hawk. I am alone by a stagnant weed-choked lake. For a moment, I see bubbles rising to the surface of the water, but it is only a trick of my imagination, only the surface scum, moving in a slight breeze. Green Willows has frightened me, as she always frightened me.

But Green Willows is gone, I tell myself as I stand and brush my skirt. All the ghosts are gone—all the hates and loves and fears and passions. They exist no more.

Except in my heart.

CHAPTER ONE

I came that first time with trepidation. I was nineteen, and this was my first job. I had to succeed; I had nowhere else to go. I could not return to Mrs. White's school for girls. Although she had let me stay on for a while after commencement, until I found a position, I knew it had been an act of kindness that she could ill afford.

I had no home. There was an aunt who lived in Brighton. It was she who had paid my tuition and had placed me in the school when my parents died. But I had not seen her in two years, and she had made her position clear enough on her last visit.

'You needn't think you'll be coming to live with me when you finish here,' she had said sternly. 'I've done my duty by you, seen that you got your education and your room and board, and it's been all I can do to afford it, too. When you get out of here, you must look out for yourself and relieve me of the burden.'

'Yes, Aunt,' I said dutifully, feeling hollow inside. At that moment, I had no idea how a woman fared for herself in nineteenth-century England.

Later, Mrs. White reassured me. 'There are ways,' she said. 'You've had a good training here, if I may say so myself, and you're not lacking in deportment. There's always someone looking for a good governess, I think.'

When the time came, Mrs. White was right; someone was looking for a governess, someone from a lovely sounding place called Green Willows.

I said good-bye to the girls at the school, and Mrs. White gave me a tearful kiss.

'God bless you, child,' she said.

'I shall write,' I promised, and then I was gone, to what fate I could not imagine. I was filled with all sorts of fears, mingled with a certain sense of excitement and, of course, a bit of curiosity. I wondered what Green Willows would be like and about the child, a girl of ten, who was to be my student; I wondered, too, about Mr. Tremayne, my employer. Our correspondence had been brief and to the point. He had offered me no commentary on the nature of the country to which I was going, what I might expect in the way of social life, or weather; nothing except that he had a child who needed tutoring, such and such was the salary he was willing to pay, and, of course, food and lodging would be provided.

Well, I told myself, settling back into the coach. You aren't going for the social life or the weather, and the pay is much better than you had ever expected it to be.

We reached Truro after dusk. It had gotten

6

cold and wet, and a chilly draft had blown through the coach as we went. There were two other travelers, an old gentleman who complained constantly of the dampness and the driver's speed and a plump, jolly farm woman who had had occasion to visit her sister for some days and was now returning home.

They both got out at Truro, and I shrank back into my corner of the coach, frightened now that my destination was near.

The window was splashed with mud and rain so that my vision was greatly obscured. What I did glimpse were patches of an alien countryside, a different landscape from the one I had known at Mrs. White's. I realized that I had been sheltered at the school. Now I would be on my own, out in the world. I had never before considered what an awesome thing that was.

At Truro, the driver stuck his head in at the window and spoke to me.

'It's a bad night out, miss,' he said, 'If you'd rather, you could put up at the inn here and go on to Helford in the morning.'

'Thank you, but I am expected tonight, so I believe I should go on,' I said. 'And I am not going to Helford. Would you put me down please at Green Willows.'

The man gave me a curious look and said, 'Green Willows? What would you be going there for? That's no place for a sweet young thing like you, miss, if you don't mind my

7

saying so. You sure you haven't made some mistake?'

'I don't believe so,' I said, his words giving me a new fear. 'No, I'm sure. Is it so lonely then at Green Willows?'

'Lonely? Oh, aye, it's that, too,' he said. 'Wait a minute.'

He said something to a woman on the porch of the inn, and she walked over to the coach. 'Here, Ruthie,' he said. 'I was told this young miss is for Helford, and now she says she wants to be put down at Green Willows.'

The woman also stared at me strangely and said, 'I think you're making a mistake, miss. If it's work you're looking for, you won't find it there. They don't take kindly to strangers up there, and more likely than not, you'll find yourself out in the rain with nothing to do but walk back here.'

'But I've already got work there,' I said. 'I've been hired as a governess.'

The man and the woman exchanged glances, and the manner in which they had spoken and the way they looked at each other made me anxious. I watched their faces, hoping for some reassurance or explanation, but none was given.

'Well, it's none of my business, I'm sure,' the woman said and backed away from the coach.

The driver took his cue from her and nodded. 'I'll drop you off along the road, miss,' he said in a businesslike tone. 'But I can't take you up the drive to the house. We coachmen don't go up the lane there, and we wouldn't be welcome if we did. Like Ruthie said, they don't take kindly to strangers there.'

I would have questioned him further, but he was in the seat. He cracked his whip over the horses, and the coach started up so suddenly that I banged my head on the window frame. There was nothing for me to do but sit back down again, my eyes glued to the window, and wait till we reached Green Willows.

As the coach rushed down the street, I could see lights in the windows of the houses we passed and glimpses of people living their daily lives, doing their homely routines. All of a sudden, there was a lump in my throat, for I had no home, and no matter how vile things might be at Green Willows, I had no place to go back to and nothing in the world but the clothes in my portmanteau and two guineas that had been a gift from Mrs. White to tide me over until I received my pay.

We left the town, and I pressed my face to the window to watch the lights fade in the distance, and there was nothing but blackness beyond the glass.

I huddled in my corner, thoroughly miserable now, and swayed as the coach rocked and banged over the road. Each creak and groan seemed to be a whispered warning of some impending evil. The wind tore at the coach; the rain lashed at the window with renewed fury.

We came over a hill. It seemed to me that the driver was whipping up his horses to an incredible speed, as if he wanted to be through this stretch of countryside as quickly as possible.

Then we were slowing, and rather abruptly the coach halted, and the driver appeared at the window.

'Here you are, miss,' he said, opening the door and offering me a hand to help me down. 'Green Willows.'

I got out, pulling my cloak close to protect me from the rain, and stared about. I could see nothing but blackness around us.

'But where is the house?' I cried, fear making me almost hysterical.

'It's over the hill there,' he said, pointing. 'You follow that path. It's closer that way than by the drive, you see. Once you come over the hill, you'll see it. Watch you don't walk into the lake.'

He did not wait for me to question him further but tipped his hat at me and leaped up into his seat. He cracked his whip again, and he was gone, rushing away into the darkness as if the demons of hell were after him.

I stood staring after him anxiously. The wind caught my cloak and sent it swirling in the air about me. The rain lashed at my face. I was alone on a deserted road, in the dark of night.

Shivering, and not from the cold alone, I lifted my portmanteau and began to walk along the path he had indicated. It led up a gentle rise and around a stand of birch trees. It seemed to me that there were voices whispering in the birches, but it was only the wind rustling the leaves.

But there was a sound that was not just the wind, a steady clip-clop, coming rapidly nearer. Someone was riding a horse this way, riding him hard, I should judge by the sound. In my present state of mind, I would hardly have been surprised to see the devil himself.

I would have stepped off the path, but the growth here was thick and dark and pressed close so that I could not see where I might be stepping.

The horse came swiftly around the bend in the path and into view. I turned, forgetting that in the dark, in my black cloak, I would be hard to see.

That movement, with my cloak suddenly billowing again in the wind, startled the horse. He gave a little frightened cry and reared on his hind legs, flailing the air with his forefeet.

I screamed at the sight of those hooves cutting the air so close to me, and someone swore. I saw a man fall from the horse to the ground. At the same time, I stepped aside, heedless of the brush that tore at my skirt, and the horse ran by me, neighing. But he stopped a few yards along the path, apparently

11

deciding the danger was past.

Having vented some of my anxiety in screaming, and having seen that this was only a man and his horse and not some demon, I too felt that the danger was past, but I could see that for the fallen rider it might not be. He lay on the ground in a crumpled heap. Alarmed, I lifted my skirts and ran toward him.

Apparently, he had only had the wind knocked out of him, for as I approached he stirred, groaned, and sat up. Shaking his head, he turned to see me. I had stopped a few feet away.

'What the devil do you think you're doing,' he demanded in a loud, angry voice. 'Scaring my horse like that. I might have been killed.'

'I'm sorry, sir,' I said, and indeed I was. 'Can I help you?'

'Thank you, no,' he said shortly and proceeded to get up. For a moment, he looked himself over carefully, feeling here and there, trying first one arm and then the other, to see if anything was broken. Except for a slight limp when he took a step, there did not seem to be any great injuries.

At last, he returned his attention to me. I had stood just where I was, not knowing what to say or do. I could not just turn and walk away, it seemed to me, and he surely did not want my assistance.

'Who in blazes are you?' he demanded, angry again now that his inspection was completed. 'And what are you doing traipsing along this path in the middle of the night?'

'I am Mary Kirkpatrick, and I am on my way to Green Willows. I was told by the coachman when he put me down that this path would lead me there.'

'Aye, that it does,' he said, studying me in a less angered manner. After a pause, he said, 'You are awfully brave now, it seems, when only a moment ago you were as skittish as my horse.'

It was true. Since my near mishap with his frightened horse, I had quite gotten over my previous fear. I could not explain to him all the circumstances that had led up to my skittishness, as he called it: the nervousness of approaching a new, and first, job, the strange dark countryside, the attitude of the coachman and the woman at the last station. All of these, as much as the horse's hooves, had made me scream, but now I was not afraid.

'I thought you were hurt,' I said.

'And that calmed you?' he asked.

I felt a little silly; it seemed as if he were making fun of me. There was a ghost of a smile at the corners of his mouth, and his eyes had an amused glint. I could only nod in affirmation.

'Well,' he said. 'As we're both going to Green Willows, and as it is getting wet standing here, we might as well go along together. Can you ride?'

'A little,' I said dubiously, glancing around at the horse, who was now waiting placidly just along the path.

'Meaning badly,' he said with a sigh. 'Well, come on then, we'll all walk.'

'It isn't . . .' I started to say it was not necessary for him to accompany me, but he interrupted.

'It isn't far anyway,' he said. He found his hat where it had fallen and slapped it once or twice on his thigh. Then he nodded at me, and we began to walk. When we got to the waiting horse, he took the reins and walked the animal along with us.

For a while, we walked in silence. The gentleman had not introduced himself or explained why he was going to Green Willows.

From time to time, I stole little glances at him, motivated by nothing more than curiosity; he was the first person connected with Green Willows that I had met.

It was mostly his clothes that led me to wonder if he were a servant. He wore a riding cloak, a nice enough one, although I could see that it was threadbare even in the dark. Beneath the cloak, I glimpsed coarse trousers and a dirty shirt; I also glimpsed a considerable breadth of chest, although he was not much over middle height.

He was neither young nor handsome; I should have guessed his age at about thirty-five. He had dark hair, quite unruly, and indeed a 'dark' face, with his deep complexion, his stern features, and his heavy brow. Before, with his brows drawn together, his eyes had looked wrathful, but now that he was no longer angry, they did not look so fierce.

We rounded the stand of trees, and suddenly, there below us was the house with the pond in front of it and the willows drooping their branches in mournful elegance. There were one or two lights in the windows, which seemed few for so big a house.

'It's a lovely house, isn't it?' I said, relieved, for I had half expected some crumbling ruin straight out of Mrs. Radcliffe's novels.

'I suppose it is,' he said offhandedly.

A little later, as if there had been no pause in our conversation, he said, 'Irish, eh? You've got no brogue.'

'I was raised in London and in Devon,' I said.

We came down the slope, around the lake. It was lovely, even in the rain and darkness, and I felt a desire to play in that gazebo on the island.

Finally, we came to the house. As we neared the front entrance, I paused. My companion stopped too, giving me a quizzical look.

'Are . . . are you expected?' I asked. I was a little embarrassed by what I should do next. If this man were coming here for a visit, I thought he would be irritated if I came in with him, and he later learned I was a servant here.

He shrugged and said, 'More or less.'

He offered nothing more, and I did not know what to say. Finally, I said, 'I am the new governess here.'

'Yes,' he said. 'I know.'

My discomfiture increased, but as it seemed that he intended to do nothing to alleviate it, I said, 'I shall go in now, then. Thank you for your company, and I am sorry about your fall.'

He made a gesture with his hand that said that the incident was nothing and gave a little bow. 'I shall be on my way to the stables.'

I gave a little sigh of relief and said, 'Oh, you are a servant here, then.'

'No,' he said soberly. 'I am Mr. Tremayne.'

I could feel my face burning crimson. In my confusion, I could not think of what to say or do. This, then, was my new employer, and I had not only caused him to fall from his horse and spoken familiarly with him but had also insulted him by calling him a servant in his own home.

'Oh,' I cried and, turning from him, ran up the steps and banged on the front door.

CHAPTER TWO

I was ushered in by a little, elderly lady in black with a white apron and a widow's cap. With her silvery colored hair and her spectacles slipped down on her nose, she reminded me a bit of Mrs. White, which was reassuring. She was, I supposed, Mrs. Tremayne, but I could not help noting that she was considerably older than the gentleman I had met outside.

'Yes, yes, come this way, please,' she said when I told her who I was. She led me into a comfortable little sitting room, which seemed all ablaze with candles and a roaring fire in the fireplace.

'You must be frozen. What a night for travel,' she said. 'And hungry, too, I've no doubt. Here, take off your shawl, and stand by the fire . . . my, you are young. He didn't say, but then, of course, he wouldn't . . .'

She brought her fluid chatter to an abrupt stop, and I had the impression that she thought she had said more than she should. I was still unnerved by my meeting with the master, and the awkward silence jangled on me.

'I . . . I met the master,' I said, only to say something.

'Master Tremayne? He's back then?' she asked quickly.

'Yes, we . . .' I could hardly say that we had strolled through the woods together, though, and now it was my turn to stop in midsentence.

'He's a lonelyish man,' she said, as if that covered everything. 'I'll tell the mistress you're here.'

'Oh, then you're not the mistress,' I blurted out.

'Me? Heavens, no, where did you get that idea? But I suppose I should have introduced myself. We see so few people, and I was that glad to see you—I'm Mrs. Duffy, the housekeeper.'

She gave me a smile that was so warm that truly all my uneasiness vanished, and I was glad to be here in this brightly lit room and by this warm fire.

'The mistress,' she said, 'is his sister, Miss Eleanor. And now, if you'll excuse me, I'd best tell her you're here.'

She went out, her skirts whispering as she walked. The house seemed still but for the crackling of the fire. I turned to stare into its flames and thought of the man I had met on the path. How could I ever face him again? But perhaps I would not have to—no doubt I would deal most often with the mistress.

His sister, Mrs. Duffy had said. Was there no wife then? Surely there must have been, as there was a child; she must have died. That would explain why he was, as the housekeeper had put it, lonelyish.

I heard a movement and turned back toward the doorway to the hall, my eyes instinctively going upward, as one's eyes do, to meet the face of a person of normal height. Mrs. Duffy had not warned me, nor had Mr. Tremayne; there was no reason why they

18

should have, I suppose, and yet in that embarrassing second or two when I had to lower my eyes down to the level of a wheelchair, I could only wish that someone had made some reference to it.

Instinctive, too, was the shrinking feelings I experienced—pity, repulsion, even curiosity, and mixed with them was an urge to show no emotion at all.

I was aware that I had shown them by the flicker of resentment—too strong a word: perhaps, disdain?—that showed in her eyes. But it was gone in an instant, and I saw not a crippled woman in a chair but a very strong-minded one who, having paused for whatever effect just within the room, now moved forward by her own efforts. I doubted very much that she would ever want someone to push the chair for her, for she gave that impression.

Mrs. Duffy had paused behind her in the doorway. She gave me a glance, encouraging, I thought, and then said to the woman, 'This is Miss Kirkpatrick, m'am. I'll bring the tea.' She disappeared down the hall.

'Sit down, Miss Kirkpatrick. I'm Eleanor Tremayne. We'll have some tea in a minute.'

'How do you do,' I said, sitting in the chair she had indicated. She wheeled herself about so that she was facing me across a little table. I watched her hands as she turned the chair; they were strong, and her wrists were thick and powerful. She did not smile easily but kept her mouth in a thin, straight line. Her hair, a dull brown color, was worn pulled sharply back from her face, adding to her masculine look.

But for all that, her eyes, while shrewd and appraising, were not unfriendly, and I thought that she welcomed a new employee with more grace than might have been necessary.

We exchanged a few desultory remarks about my journey, plainly making conversation until the tea was brought in. In a moment, Mrs. Duffy returned, bearing a silver tray that she placed in front of Miss Tremayne. I had been wondering if I would meet Mr. Tremayne again; I rather hoped not, as I thought I would be embarrassed to face him so soon after my faux pas. Apparently, though, I was to be spared that awkwardness, as there were only the two cups on the tray.

She poured, all the while asking me polite questions: I was an orphan, wasn't I? Had I no relatives at all, then? How long had I been at Mrs. White's? Had I been to this part of the country before?

I answered her questions as openly and as pleasantly as possible. She had, after all, every right to know everything about me, and in fact, my correspondence with her brother, which had led to my being hired, had not included a great many questions regarding my background, so that much of what she asked me was, from their point of view, new territory.

But as I sipped my tea, I found it increasingly difficult to follow the conversation. I had traveled all day, most of it in a cold rain. The warmth of the fire combined with the warmth of the tea and made me drowsy, and I found myself making an effort to keep my eyes open.

I must have actually begun to nod my head, for she said abruptly, breaking off some sentence, the direction of which I had lost, 'Why, how thoughtless of me. You're tired, of course.'

I brought my head up with a jerk and said as quickly as I could, 'Oh, no, it's all right, really.'

'Nonsense,' she said, dismissing my protests with a quick gesture. 'Would you ring for Mrs. Duffy—that cord over there, just by the door—thank you.'

I went to the cord as asked and pulled it, hearing a faint tinkling sound in the distance. In a moment, Mrs. Duffy bustled in, and at Miss Tremayne's instructions, I was escorted off to my room.

As we were going out, though, she asked me something that struck me as odd. 'Miss Kirkpatrick,' she said, as we started into the hall, 'are you a fanciful girl?'

I paused, looking back at her. It was such an unexpected question that I had to think for a moment before answering.

'Why, I don't know,' I said.

'You don't know?'

21

'At Mrs. White's, there was hardly any opportunity for being fanciful.'

'I see,' she said, those shrewd eyes of hers studying me so intensely that I had to resist an urge to fidget. 'Well, we shall have to hope that you are not.' She paused and in a lower voice added, 'If you should have the opportunity.'

I hesitated a few seconds more, but she had lowered her gaze and was studying her hands; apparently I was dismissed. When I glanced at Mrs. Duffy, she gave me a faint smile and led the way from the room, and I was obliged to follow her.

As she led me up the stairs, Mrs. Duffy kept up a steady stream of chatter, a nervous sort of chatter that sprang, I guessed, from her pleasure at having an audience. It did not, fortunately, require much in the way of answers from me, for I found myself looking around with curiosity, examining my new surroundings.

It was a striking house, far more luxurious than anything I had been in before. At the same time, though, there was an artificiality about the place that jarred; it had a contrived look of oldness, but it was apparent at second glance that the house was really rather new. Mrs. White's, for instance, had originally been a manor house and went back several hundred years, while I would not have guessed Green Willows to be more than, say, twenty or thirty years old.

Yet for all its newness, the house had an odd air of neglect, of disuse. I do not mean that it was dirty or shabby; the light from Mrs. Duffy's lamp gleamed smartly on silver and brass and freshly washed mirrors. The walls were paneled partway up in a very handsome if dark wood, and a rich brocade cloth covered above that. But there was an emptiness, a hollow quality; when one spoke, one's voice rang falsely on the air. It was like a house that, although kept up, has not been lived in for many years.

But I thought that perhaps I was being fanciful indeed, and at any rate, I was glad to see that I would be living in such a fine house.

The stairs were wide and thickly carpeted. They went up straight to a landing and then off at right angles in either direction. As we reached the landing, the light showed a handsome portrait hanging there; in daylight, it would dominate the stairs.

'Oh,' I said, pausing involuntarily. 'How lovely.'

'Who? Oh, that, yes,' Mrs. Duffy said, pausing too. 'That was the missus, his wife—the little girl's mother. She is lovely, isn't she? Her name was Angela, and they say that's exactly like what she was, an angel.'

She lifted the lamp so that its light fell directly on the portrait and revealed a slim, pale woman in a white gown, her creamy yellow hair tumbling about her face and shoulders. The artist had created for her a dreamlike setting of clouds and golden rays of light, and he had blended cloud and gown, light and hair, to make of his model a creature not only human but a thing of gossamer and light and dreams—an angel, truly, with that heavenly smile, those gentle, loving eyes.

I could hardly picture her as the wife of the man I had met on the path, who seemed so rough, so inelegant.

But the portrait had put my mind at ease on one point. I need not worry about the nature of the girl I was going to be teaching; with such a mother, could the child be anything but an angel herself?

I said as much to Mrs. Duffy as we continued on our way, and she smiled and said, 'Little Elizabeth, aye, she's an angel all right, never you worry about her, miss.'

'Is her mother deceased?'

'Yes, some years ago, they say. But folks around here can't talk nice enough about her.'

'Did you know her?' I asked. We had reached the upper corridor, and I was led quickly toward the rear of the house.

'Me? Oh, no, miss, I've only been here a few months. And it's lonesome, I don't mind saying. I'll be glad for your company.'

'And I for yours, I'm sure,' I said. We had reached a closed door, which she swung open for me. 'This is my first employment, you know.'

24

'Is it now? And you've come all the way here to Green Willows. There, I think you'll like this room, miss. I've lighted the fires, and there's a warming pan for you.'

It was a small but cozy room, with a four-poster bed, a dressing table, a small wooden chair by the fire, and bright curtains at the windows.

'It's lovely,' I said, not daring to tell her how it compared to the shabby cubbyhole I had had at Mrs. White's. 'You certainly do seem to do everything, though.'

'I do what has to be done, miss,' she said with an odd note of pique in her voice.

'Are there no other servants, then?' I asked, putting my shawl on the back of the chair. My bag, I saw, had been brought up.

'Not just now,' she said. She took the pillows from the bed and began to fluff them.

The change in her manner struck an uneasy chord within me, and I began to think again of the strange warnings of the coach driver and the woman at the inn. I was tired and susceptible, and suddenly, I began to worry again.

Trying to still the worrisome voice within me, I said, 'I suppose it's a long walk from the village.'

'Oh, that,' she said. 'I walk it myself twice a week. No, we've got no shortage of help during the days.' She paused, pounding the pillow with such ferocity that I have expected it to burst and scatter a flurry of feathers about the room.

She added, quickly, 'They won't stay nights. There, I think that'll be comfortable for you.'

'Mrs. Duffy,' I said on a rising note, 'is there anything wrong with Green Willows, with the Tremaynes?'

'Wrong?' She looked flustered, and I could see that she was embarrassed by my question, even though she had perhaps prompted it. She was a well-trained servant and as such knew the importance of loyalty to her employer. 'Why, what on earth could have given you that idea, miss? They're very fine people, I'm sure, and as for Green Willows, why it's a lovely home, if it is a bit lonely.'

'Is it so isolated, then?' I asked, my anxiety hardly laid to rest. 'Are there no visitors?'

'Visitors, miss? To Green Willows?' Her expression made this seem so incongruous that my fears were again fanned into flame. But she would not let me voice them.

'Now, miss,' she said in a soothing tone, 'you're tired, I expect, and you're letting your imagination run away with you. What you want is a good night's sleep.'

'But I . . .'

'If you need anything, all you've got to do is pull that cord there,' she said, effectively silencing any further questions I might have. 'Good night, miss. You'll feel better in the morning.'

With that, she left, but not before pausing in the doorway to say again, 'I'm that glad you're here, miss.'

I was left alone in my room. The fire crackled on the grate, and the wind rattled the shutters. I went to the window and looked out, but I could see little. Apparently, we were right on the headland, as the earth seemed simply to drop away a hundred yards or so from the house. Although the grounds in front were beautifully landscaped, here it appeared that the darkness lay upon a barren hillside except for one old, gnarled tree that stood near the cliff's edge, its branches twisted into a grotesque attitude of beseeching.

But for all my worries, Mrs. Duffy was right. I was tired, and having thrown the bolt on my door, a perhaps unnecessary gesture that nonetheless gave me a greater peace of mind, I was soon into my bed and, grateful for the warming pan, asleep in no more than a few minutes.

*   *   *

I do not know how long I slept before I was awakened. The fire had burned down to a few glowing coals, and the room was cold. Outside the wind still rattled the shutters and thrust one icy draft across the floor of the room.

For a moment, I lay still muffled in sleep, trying to recall first where I was and then why I had awakened. Then I heard it again—a distant sound of sobbing.

I thought at once of my new pupil, Elizabeth. Was she crying in her bed, perhaps even because I was here? Some girls did so resent education, I knew. Perhaps to her, I represented a loss of freedom or a loss of the time she might otherwise spend with her father or her aunt, although I could not imagine Eleanor Tremayne comfortable in the presence of children.

Hardly thinking, I slipped from my room and went to the door. I could hear the crying more clearly here; yes, it was a girl's voice and not far away, I thought. I slid back the bolt and opened the door, stepping into the hallway. A distant candle or a lamp burned around a corner, giving the faintest of glows to the hall, which was empty.

I went back for my dressing gown, slipping quickly into it, and came into the hall again. I turned and gave a little startled cry as someone moved just a few feet from me.

'Mr. Tremayne,' I breathed, so relieved to find it was only him that I was not embarrassed at being found in the dark hall, in my dressing gown. 'You startled me.'

'I shouldn't wonder,' he said, coming to stand directly in front of me. Those hard eyes stared down at me. 'Is something wrong, Miss Kirkpatrick?'

'It was that sobbing,' I said. 'It woke me, and

28

I came to see what was wrong.'

For a long moment, he continued to stare at me. I cannot say that his face was expressionless; indeed, it seemed full of expression, but of what, I could not read.

'What sobbing?' he asked finally.

'Why, the sound of crying . . .' I stopped. Except for our voices, whispering, the house lay still about us. 'But, it . . . I heard it. You must have heard it too,' I said, feeling as if that icy draft of air were moving up my spine.

'I heard nothing but your door open,' he said. 'I came to see what was wrong.'

I could think of nothing to say, nor could I meet his unwavering gaze. I looked down, suddenly conscious of my dishabille, of the lateness of the hour, and of how foolish I must look.

'This is an oddly constructed house, Miss Kirkpatrick,' he said, speaking as one might speak to a child. 'And the wind comes straight in from the sea. Sometimes it makes strange noises. You'll get used to them.'

'No doubt I will,' I said, backing into my room. 'I'm sorry to have bothered you.'

'No bother,' he said, not moving. 'Good night. Are you comfortable in this room?'

'Very, thank you.'

'You met my sister?'

'Yes, she was most gracious.'

'Well, then, good night.'

'Good night,' I said and closed the door. I

wondered if he listened and heard as I slid the bolt into place. I did not hear him walk away, although I remained leaning against the door for some minutes, ears straining.

At length, I went back to the welcome warmth of my bed and pulled the covers up to my chin. But I did not fall asleep so quickly this time. I lay for a long while, listening to the sounds of the wind.

But it did not sob again, and eventually, I fell asleep.

CHAPTER THREE

I woke to a morning that lay shining and splendid over the green hills and the distant sea below us. The wind had become a gentle breeze, the rain had vanished, and with it had vanished my fears and apprehensions.

Soon after I had awakened, and unbolted my door, a thin, nervous little girl in a maid's outfit came in with a tray on which rested a pot of tea and some bread.

'If you please, miss,' she said, making an awkward little curtsey. 'Miss Duffy thought you might enjoy some tea this morning, and the master says when you're up and about could he see you in the library?'

'Thank you. I'll be down shortly,' I said. 'But you mustn't treat me like a guest, I'm an employee too, and I hope we can be friends. My name is Mary.'

'Thank you, miss,' she said, but with no great warmth. 'I'm Daisy. I'm here days, during the week, you understand.'

'Yes, Mrs. Duffy said no one stayed nights. For a while, I was getting afraid—you know, imagining all sorts of foolish things.' I gave a little laugh to show how I now regarded this. But Daisy did not laugh or even smile; she only gave me a curious sideways glance and then looked away.

'If you'll excuse me, miss, I've got plenty to do,' she said, and she was gone before I could say anything more, scurrying away as if afraid of me, which led me to conclude that Daisy was probably afraid of everything, and so I need not mind what she thought about things. Still, some of the sparkle had gone out of the morning.

After a slight moment of uncertainty, I found the library and Mr. Tremayne waiting there. He was looking out the window, hands folded behind his back. He was dressed rather more elegantly than before, although his clothes were still somewhat old-fashioned and just a bit threadbare.

He heard me come in and turned to regard me. There was nothing friendly about his look—I thought of a fierce bear I had seen once in a traveling show. Indeed, he scowled so fiercely that I could not but think I had done something wrong and wondered if he were angry that I had left my room during the night.

I was about to speak, to offer an apology, when at last he addressed me.

'Miss Kirkpatrick,' he said. 'I don't know how much my sister may have said to you last night.'

He paused; was that a question? Not knowing, I chose silence, being somewhat intimidated by his gruff manner.

'You have been teaching?' he asked.

'Yes, at a girls' school.'

'At . . .' he paused and glanced down at a letter that he had picked up and that I saw was mine. 'At Mrs. White's.' I nodded. 'My daughter is ten. I believe I told you that.'

'Yes,' I said. I had grown more puzzled than frightened by this hemming and hawing. I saw that he wanted to say something but was not sure how to go about it, and close on the heels of this observation came the realization that his gruff manner was a sign not of unfriendliness or disapproval, as I had thought, but of a shy reserve. He felt as awkward with me as I did with him, and that realization suddenly put me completely at my ease with him.

'Perhaps it would be best if I met your daughter,' I said, trying to help him through what I could now see was a difficult interview.

He looked relieved at having the direction

of the interview taken from his hands and said, 'You may be right. I'll take you to meet her this morning.'

'Take me to meet her? She isn't here, then?'

Again I had that feeling of awkwardness, of things that needed to be said but somehow could not be said.

'My daughter does not live at Green Willows, Miss Kirkpatrick,' he said after a pause. 'She lives in the village with her grandfather, Commander Whittsett. Unfortunately, his cottage is too small to accommodate you there, which is why you must continue to live at Green Willows. I trust that that arrangement will be satisfactory to you?'

'Of course, as you wish. And will I teach her here or . . .'

'You will teach her at her grandfather's cottage. The village is not far if you want to walk each day, or there is a trap. If you'd prefer, I can have someone drive you to and from . . .'

'No, that won't be necessary,' I said. 'I'm accustomed to walking; indeed, I like a walk each day.'

A silence fell. I could not think what I could say to break it. Surely, I could not ask the questions that were on my mind—but I could not help wondering about the living arrangements that kept the daughter in the village and her father and her governess here at Green Willows. It might well be true that her grandfather's cottage was too small for me to live there, but surely, there was more than enough room for her to live here at Green Willows. And that was the customary thing, was it not?

But he offered no answers to these questions, although be must be aware that they were on my mind. He said, brusquely, 'If you'd like, we can go now.'

'I'll get my things,' I said, turning to go.

'There's no real hurry, of course,' he said. 'If you'd rather have a day to rest from your travels.'

'I think the sooner I meet your daughter, the better,' I said. 'And I am quite rested, thank you.'

'You slept well then?'

Despite myself, I paused and glanced back, and our eyes met. 'Yes,' I said. 'After . . . that one difficulty.'

'You will get used to Green Willows,' he said.

To that, I could say nothing. It was certainly not a point on which, just now, I was willing to agree with him, and I left him to fetch my things.

*   *   *

The village was so near that it hardly justified hitching horse to rig, and I told Mr. Tremayne so. It was our first conversation since I had rejoined him, and we had started into town.

'It can't be more than a fifteen-minute walk,' I said.

'About that,' he said. 'Although Mrs. Duffy manages to stretch it to an hour or so. But I suspect she stops along the way to visit with friends.'

'She has local friends, then,' I said, rather without thinking. 'She seemed a little lonely, I thought.'

'Green Willows can be a lonely place,' he said. 'I have been a little concerned about that in view of your youth. Perhaps it will weigh a bit too heavily upon you.'

'I am not unaccustomed to loneliness,' I said.

He sounded surprised when he said, 'I should have thought that at a girls' school . . . ?'

'One can be lonely and surrounded by people.'

'How true,' he said with such vehemence that I wondered again about the depth of feeling he hid behind his taciturn manner.

I stole a sideways glance at him, but I do not think he noticed me in more than a superficial manner, any more than he really noticed the task of driving the rig. His attention was turned elsewhere, inward, and I could only puzzle at what vistas he contemplated there. What passions, what furies, had driven him within himself, hiding within the rough walls of his seemingly unfriendly personality, just as he hid his physical self within the walls of Green Willows?

He said, quite unexpectedly, 'You are a remarkable girl, Miss Kirkpatrick.'

I was completely flustered by the remark and could have given no answer to it, but fortunately, none was necessary, as we seemed to have arrived at our destination. The road had taken us directly into the village along its one street, with cottages and shops along either side. Halfway through the town, the road separated, one branch leading down to the sea, where I could see a little cluster of boats bobbing on the water's surface, and the other road leading slightly uphill.

We had taken the uphill road, which now ended before a little cottage. Mr. Tremayne stopped before it and, alighting, came around to hand me down.

This was a charming cottage, with a lovely view of the sea, although I could well believe there was not enough room for me to live there. It was a tiny, white clapboard structure with a thatched roof and blue shutters. I thought a curtain fluttered at one of the windows as I climbed down from the rig, but when I glanced again, it was still, and I could not say for certain whether or not someone was watching.

He used the knocker rather forcefully, and almost at once, the door was opened by a pretty little girl of about ten, looking altogether awed by our visit. Her eyes, like little delft saucers, went from him to me and back again with an air both of fear and barely repressed excitement.

'My grandfather is not here,' she said, stepping back so that we might enter. 'He has gone down to the harbor, but he shall be back in a few minutes. Would you like me to fetch him?'

'That won't be necessary; we'll wait in the parlor,' Mr. Tremayne said, leading the way into a diminutive little room off the hall. It was blue and white, with dark wooden beams on the ceiling and a great deal of brass everywhere, which gave it a nautical flavor. On the mantle over the fireplace was a large bottle containing a complete model of a ship, and there were several seafaring prints on the wall.

In short, it was a man's room, but it was bright and sunny, and the windows looked down upon the little harbor with its brightly colored boats. I hoped that we could have our lessons here.

That this girl was Elizabeth, I felt certain, but I was struck by the restraint between father and daughter; hardly a word had been spoken beyond that first, cold exchange. We had seated ourselves, Mr. Tremayne and I, in two chairs near the window, and the girl had taken a stiff-looking wooden chair facing us. She sat with her feet properly together, her hands folded neatly in her lap, but I could still see the air of barely contained excitement, and her eyes, which were the only part of her moving just now, went continually from her father to me.

The silence grew oppressive. I could hear the steady tick tock of a grandfather's clock in the hall, and a fly buzzed impudently about my head. There was a scent of old spices to the room and a tang of sea air, and something else that at first I could not identify but finally recognized as gardenia. I decided the girl was wearing a scent and wondered if her father approved at her young age.

The door opened suddenly, breaking into the stillness so sharply that I started. But neither father nor daughter noticed me, for their eyes had gone at once to the archway that led to the hall, and I too looked in that direction just as a tall, weather-beaten man appeared in it. He had pewter-colored hair and eyes not much darker, which now swept the room coldly, settling on me.

Mr. Tremayne had risen as the commander entered, and in way of introduction, he said, 'This is the new governess.'

'Damn fool nonsense,' was the disdainful reply.

I had started to rise, but at this, I thought better of it and settled stiffly back into my seat, my face coloring slightly.

'We'd better talk in here,' Mr. Tremayne said, leading the way out of the room. With another icy scowl about the parlor, as if he suspected I had been purloining his ships' fittings, the commander followed him.

Elizabeth and I were left alone, and again he silence descended, although I could hear the men's voices faintly in the distance, the commander's occasionally rising sharply on some obscenity.

'I'm Mary Kirkpatrick,' I said, addressing the girl for the first time. 'I'm to be your new governess.'

'I know,' she said. She smiled, bringing her face to such life that at last she looked like the girl she was and not the little old woman she had been imitating. 'If Grandfather allows it.'

'I can't see why he would not,' I said, more sharply than I intended.

She bit her lip, and I could see that she was torn between making some reply to this or keeping silent. I was about to say that, of course, he knew the situation better than I did when she spoke again.

'He wants me sent away to school,' she said. 'Somewhere far away, to France maybe.'

I thought it peculiar that nothing of this had been said to me and that I had been hired and brought into the middle of this conflict before it was properly resolved, as if Mr. Tremayne had been trying to provide a fait accompli.

Aloud, I said diplomatically, 'Perhaps he has reasons for thinking that best.'

She suddenly jumped up from her chair and

came across to me, dropping to one knee so that she could look me straight into the face. She lowered her voice to a conspiratorial whisper.

'Oh, he has his reasons, all right. He wants to keep me away from Green Willows,' she said. 'He would do anything to keep me from there.'

The remark, so unlike anything I had been prepared for, struck a responsive chord in my own uneasiness, which I quickly tried to quell.

'Don't you like Green Willows?' I asked.

'Like it?' She looked aghast at the suggestion, as if I had wounded her to the quick. 'Oh, Miss Kirkpatrick, if you only knew. I love Green Willows. I want to go back. You've got to help me, help me persuade them to let me come home to Green Willows.'

'Why, I . . .' I stammered, nonplussed. 'Surely, if your father and your grandfather both want you here, why . . . but there must be a reason.'

'They're trying to keep me from my mother,' she said.

At that moment, we heard their steps in the hall. In a twinkling, she had leaped up and regained her chair, and when the two men came into the room, they found us as before, I with my face a little reddened, she seated demurely in her wooden chair, her expression one of innocent—although hesitant—expectancy.

I could not but wonder exactly what she was

expecting of me.

CHAPTER FOUR

I do not know what conversation passed between Mr. Tremayne and Commander Whittsett, but the result of it was that it was agreed I would begin lessons with Elizabeth the following morning, which seemed to please Elizabeth greatly, although she was careful to remain restrained.

I was properly introduced to her and to the commander, who acknowledged me grudgingly. 'I think it only fair to tell you,' he said, 'that I was and am opposed to bringing a governess in here for my granddaughter. I believe she should be sent away to a proper school. But I have agreed to go along with this arrangement for the time being. Later, we shall see.'

'I shall do my best to produce the results you desire,' I said. 'But that shall be easier if I know exactly what they are.'

He looked a bit taken aback by my boldness, as he no doubt had a right to be. I thought I saw a fleeting smile on Mr. Tremayne's face, although I could not imagine what he found amusing. His daughter looked surprised, for, I suppose, no one ever spoke up to the commander. Indeed, I was not a little frightened of him myself, but I believe in facing up to things. If I were to please him, and I thought that I would have to do that to retain my position, I must know what he had in mind.

'Why, what I desire,' he said, 'is to see my granddaughter properly educated and to see her kept from any unhealthy influences.'

This reply was so patently rude that I quite forgot my promise to myself to keep my Irish temper 'on the shelf.' 'Well, sir,' I said, 'As to her education, I have come from a school that has a fine reputation and teaches the latest methods, and I shall endeavor to give your granddaughter as good an education as she would get there, which is to say as good an education as she could get anywhere. And as for the other, I truly hope that neither she nor you will find me an unhealthy influence.'

I do not know what I expected in the way of a response to this, but now that I had spoken, my temper had cooled somewhat so that I would not have considered it surprising or inappropriate if he had struck me with a bolt of lightning.

He did not answer for a long moment, and this time the room's silence was quite ominous. I supposed that I would be dismissed on the spot and was already thinking ahead to my ignominious return to Mrs. White's.

'I did not mean to imply that you were an unhealthy influence,' he said, speaking coolly. 'And as to your credentials, I have no doubt they are impeccable, else my son-in-law would not have hired you for the job. I believe I can trust him in that.'

I think be would have said something more, probably about my manners, but Mr. Tremayne intervened, stepping quickly to my side and taking my arm.

'Then if everything's settled, we'll go now,' he said. 'Miss Kirkpatrick will take up her duties in the morning, as we've agreed.'

He propelled me in the direction of the door, himself lingering behind to say something to his father-in-law. I heard the commander say, 'She's spunky,' but whether he added that this pleased or displeased him, I could not hear; I suspected the latter.

My employer was no more talkative on the way home than he had been coming in, although I was aware that once or twice he turned to study my profile. If my position in the household had been tentative before, I could not help but admit it was more so now, and I wondered if he were regretting his impulsiveness in hiring me just as I was regretting my impulsiveness in speaking my mind so frankly.

I was not sorry, though, for a free day to unwind a bit and settle into my new—if perhaps temporary—home. I sought out Mrs. Duffy in the kitchen, where she was supervising the planning of the meals for the next few days. The cook, a stout, commanding presence who seemed happy enough to meet me, was the only other full-time servant, and she returned to her own home at sundown each night, so that meals at Green Willows had to be taken early or served cold.

'You get used to it, though,' Mrs. Duffy said cheerfully. 'It's quiet here in the evenings, and you'll be glad enough to go to bed early.'

I inquired about my meals, thinking that I was to take them in the kitchen, but she informed me that I would take them with the master and mistress in the dining room. I was rather of two minds about this. It was flattering to discover that my station was somewhat above that of a common servant. On the other hand, I was inclined to think I would enjoy a meal in the kitchen more, in the cook's frank presence.

As it turned out, I had lunch alone in the dining room, Mr. Tremayne being out somewhere, Mrs. Duffy did not say where, and Miss Tremayne, having a headache, staying to her room. I had some soup and a bit of trifle, served by the same timorous girl who had come to my room that morning. She was no more receptive to my overtures of friendship than she had been before, and I began to think that life at Green Willows was perhaps going to be as lonely as everyone said.

I could only wonder why young Elizabeth, who, I thought, away from her grandfather's rather frightening presence would no doubt be as gay and frolicsome as any young girl, should want to live here rather than in that sunny, bright cottage in the village.

I climbed the stairs to my room, pausing at the landing to stare again at the portrait of the dead Mrs. Tremayne. I found my eyes going to those in the portrait, and for a moment, it seemed as if those painted eyes were looking into mine, as if they had come to life and were trying to tell me something, some message that I could not grasp.

I had never been a particularly fanciful person, though, and now I mentally shook myself, making myself move up the stairs and away from that painted gaze.

As I did so, I heard a sound, faintly at first and then more distinctly—the sound of someone humming. I did not know the song, but it had a catchy, easy to remember quality—a folk song of some sort, I thought. It was coming from the hall above, and when I reached there, I heard it coming quite clearly from one of the rooms past mine.

My first thought was that it was one of the maids, but when I thought of Daisy, I could not imagine her humming this happy little tune. Perhaps Eleanor Tremayne, recovered from her headache? But then I caught the scent of gardenias and realized with pleasure that Elizabeth must have come to Green Willows on some crrand—maybe her father and grandfather had, after all, decreed that

45

she could stay here now that she had a governess.

I was quite delighted, for, although her behavior had been a little odd this morning, I had an impression that she was a thoroughly likeable young lady, and I was looking forward to our lessons.

I followed the humming—it was odd how clearly it carried along the hall—and came at last to a door at the very end of the corridor, the last room along this way. The sound was clearly coming from just inside the room, and I knocked lightly before reaching to open the door.

The door was locked. The humming had stopped, and from within, I had the impression of someone waiting, holding her breath, listening. It gave me an odd, uncomfortable chill so that I tapped again, a trifle impatiently.

'What are you doing there?' someone demanded sharply.

I whirled about, feeling guilty for no reason I could have explained, and saw Eleanor Tremayne just along the hall. A door was open on what I took to be her bedroom; apparently, she had come out to investigate my tapping.

'Why, I . . . I heard something,' I said, stumbling over my own tongue.

I heard a sharp intake of breath, and she wheeled her chair along the hall toward me. 'You heard something in there?' she asked.

'Someone humming,' I said. 'I thought it

was Elizabeth, and . . .'

'Humming? From in there?' she asked, interrupting me.

'I thought so, but it's stopped.'

She reached for the knob and gave it a good yank. 'It's locked,' she said, as if accusing me of locking it.

'I know. I must have been mistaken. I am sorry.'

'There's no one in there,' she said shortly. 'There never is.'

'Of course,' I said.

She wheeled her chair about to return down the hall, but she paused and turned back to me. 'Never go to that room,' she said.

'Very well,' I said, since it seemed I must say something.

She went quickly along to her room, but when she reached the door and might have gone inside, she again looked back at me.

'You must have been mistaken,' she said in a less hostile voice. 'You must have heard the wind.'

To this, I did not reply, and she did not wait for one but went inside, closing her door firmly, leaving me to walk slowly, thoughtfully, back to my own room.

*   *   *

By dinner time, Eleanor seemed to have forgotten the incident entirely. At least she did

47

not mention it, and she was in a far more genial mood.

The three of us—Mr. Tremayne, Miss Tremayne, and myself—were alone at the huge old dining table. Mrs. Duffy herself served, bustling to and fro with a variety of delicious and well-prepared food. Cook might be as stubborn as everyone else about staying overnight, but she gave good value for her pay when she was here.

'You've met my niece, I understand,' Eleanor said as the main course was being served.

'Yes. I found her quite charming,' I said. 'And she gives the impression she's quite bright.'

'You'll have no difficulty with Elizabeth regarding her lessons,' Eleanor said.

I decided to take the bull by the horns, so to speak, and I looked along the table to where the master sat. He had as yet taken no part in the conversation and had said nothing since wishing me good evening.

'I can't help thinking,' I said, 'that it would be a great deal easier if Elizabeth were allowed to come here. And I feel that she wants to. Surely, now that I am here, and she would have supervision . . .'

But I had to stop. Mr. Tremayne had looked down the table at me, and his look was so cold, so displeased, that whatever I was going to say died on my lips, and I found myself speechless.

To my embarrassment, my hand, holding my water goblet, trembled slightly.

'My daughter lives with her grandfather,' he said, speaking slowly and firmly. 'She will take her lessons there. I thought that was understood.'

'Yes, of course,' I said. I waited, but after glowering at me for a moment more, he returned his attention to his dinner. I picked up my fork and stabbed my mutton.

CHAPTER FIVE

The following morning, I strolled into the village for my first lesson with Elizabeth. Mrs. Duffy had asked me to run an errand for her, so I stopped in the kitchen before setting out.

'The vicar's sister lives with him, and she supplies our eggs,' Mrs. Duffy explained. 'We'll need a dozen, if you don't mind stopping there on your way home and just picking them up. Besides, she'll be dying of curiosity about you by this time, and it'll give her as good a chance as any to meet you.'

'I'm afraid she'll be disappointed,' I said, laughing. 'How do I know the house?'

'You can't miss it if you take the path down about the lake and follow that to the road; it's the first cottage along the road. I'd go myself, but me legs have been bothering me a bit.'

49

'And besides it would deprive the vicar's sister of her opportunity to meet me,' I said.

It was a pleasant stroll. I had seen the path and the lake before by night, but they were even lovelier in the day. Someone had laid out the grounds with an eye for studied beauty, and I was struck by the contrast between this view and the one behind the house, the hill sloping downward to that stark cliff with the single wind-twisted tree to accentuate rather than relieve the bleakness.

When I was closer, though, I saw that the atmosphere of disuse that I had sensed in the house was even stronger here. Mrs. Duffy's busy hands had not reached this far, and I could see that the grounds were being allowed to go to ruin. Walks needed trimming, shrubs had started to go wild, a sundial had been overturned, perhaps by some rowdy youths, and allowed to lie on its side.

There was a little bridge that arched across the water to the island in the lake, and I went over it, noting that while the wood still looked sound it had been a long while since it had been painted. The little gazebo on the island was black with dirt and dust, but cleaned up, it would be a delightful place to wile away a few hours with a book, listening to the sough of the water on the shore.

But time was passing, and if I wanted to make a good impression on Commander Whittsett, which I thought was essential to my staying on, I had better not start by being late.

I was on time, but I do not think my punctuality made any difference in the commander's disapproval of me. He bade me a rather stony welcome and saw me into the bright parlor with its view of the harbor, where we were to have our lessons. I had expected that he might sit in on the first few at least to see for himself what skill I might possess, but having entrusted his granddaughter to me, the commander left the house and did not return until just before the appointed quitting time. I was rather relieved, as I feared that his stern presence might have inhibited Elizabeth as well as myself.

Once he had gone, Elizabeth again went through her transformation, becoming a bright, spontaneous girl as she should have been. From time to time, the housekeeper came in, but her presence apparently did not inhibit the child.

We got on quite well. Elizabeth's education had been neglected up till now, and she was not so far along as a girl her age would have been at Mrs. White's, but she was obviously bright and eager to learn, and I felt confident that within a few weeks her progress would be the best argument for my tutorship.

On that first day, I tried to cover all the subjects that we would be doing, to get a picture of where she was in relation to them. Finally, I gave her a number of arithmetic problems and set her to work. While she worked, I took up my own book to read.

I was only gradually aware that while Elizabeth worked she was humming softly to herself. It was such an inconsequential sound that I would perhaps not have noticed it at all had the song not intruded itself upon my memory. I listened for a moment, trying to place it, and finally, it came to me—this was the song I had heard someone humming in the upstairs hall at Green Willows—behind the locked door of a room that had been forbidden to me.

'Elizabeth, what is that song?' I asked.

She gave me a curious look and said, 'I don't know the name or the words, just the melody.'

'Where do you know it from?'

She hesitated, and I think she was reluctant to tell me the truth. But at last she said, in an almost defiant tone, 'My mother used to hum it when I was very little.'

As she said this, her hand, in an apparently involuntary gesture, crumpled the paper on which she had been working her arithmetic problems. I remembered then her strange remarks that other day when I had been here, to the effect that her grandfather and father were trying to keep her away from Green Willows and away from her mother. Perhaps she had been forbidden to speak of her mother. Perhaps she had even been forbidden to hum this little song.

'Oh, my dear,' I said, standing and going to her. 'I'm not objecting to the song; it's a very pretty song. I was only curious, that's all. I heard someone humming it just yesterday.'

'That song?' she asked, startled. 'Where?'

'At Green Willows.'

Her expression was one of incredulity. 'Who was humming it?' she asked.

'I don't know, I was . . . interrupted before I saw who it was. But I'm certain it was the same song.'

'No one there would be singing that song. They all hated her—my father, my aunt . . .'

'That surely isn't true,' I protested, but even to my own ears I sounded unconvinced.

'That's why they won't let me go to Green Willows. They don't want me to remember her, they don't want me to see any reminders of her, they don't even want me to talk to anyone about her. They think I'll forget she ever lived.'

'Elizabeth,' I said. Her fervent tone of voice was oddly chilling.

'She was an angel, just like her name,' she said, suddenly beaming up at me with a passionate look. 'I'm not supposed to talk to anyone about her, but I have, to people here in the town, and they all say the same thing. They say she was beautiful and good and kind. I worship her, and they're so hateful to keep me from her like this.'

She began suddenly to cry. Here at least was something I could understand and cope with. I knew what it was like to lose a parent when you are very young. It was easy then to idolize them, and I thought that in trying to erase the memory of her mother from Elizabeth's consciousness her father had accomplished just the opposite, making an obsession of her. It would be far better, in my opinion, to allow the child to come to Green Willows, to see her mother's things, to talk to people about her, and to remember her in a more healthy fashion.

I put an arm about her thin shoulders and said comfortingly, 'I do understand. I lost my own mother when I was a young girl, and even now I feel the loss. But in time, you will get used to it, believe me.'

She turned a tear-stained face to me. 'It would be easier,' she said, 'if they'd let me come to Green Willows. Couldn't you ask them?'

'I doubt that it would do any good. I tried to speak to your father about it last night, and he seemed quite adamant. No doubt there is some reason for his attitude.'

'Will you try again?' she pleaded.

'I . . , well, I can't promise you anything,' I said, not wanting to let her down too cruelly. 'If the opportunity seems to present itself, yes, I'll try to talk to him again. But you mustn't expect too much. He really did not seem to welcome the subject.'

She seemed satisfied with that, and I had begun to hope that we could return to safer ground, when she asked, 'Miss Kirkpatrick . . .'

'Mary,' I corrected her.

'Mary, would you do something for me?'

'I shall certainly try, if you'll tell me what it is,' I said.

'Would you . . . go to her room and get me something of hers?' I started to protest, and she went on quickly, 'Oh, it needn't be anything special, just a piece of ribbon or something like that. And they really should have become mine, shouldn't they have, so it wouldn't be like you were stealing, would it?'

I was about to say that I could not do what she asked, but she looked so very hopeful that I was afraid the disappointment might spoil any rapport that had been established between us; so instead, I said lamely, 'I shall see, but again I can make no promises. Which room is hers, by the way?'

'It's the last one along the hall,' Elizabeth said. 'Upstairs.'

I think it was then that I first began to realize what the trouble was at Green Willows.

CHAPTER SIX

'Something happened up at Green Willows,' Elizabeth said.

'What do you mean? What happened?' I asked. We were finished with the lessons. Through the window, I could see the commander marching uphill toward the cottage, shoulders square, chin high. Several people greeted him from doorways and windows, and he acknowledged each of them with a faint suggestion of a nod, but he neither paused nor turned his head.

'I don't know. It was a long time ago, when I was little,' she said. 'That's why they won't let me come there, I think. But if it happened so long ago, what harm could it do now?'

'Elizabeth,' I said, speaking quickly, as the commander was almost home now. 'I will do what I can with your father. I promise I will speak to him. But you must promise to keep this conversation to yourself and not to try to talk to anyone else about these things.'

'I promise,' she said.

'And to work very hard at your lessons,' I added, almost as an afterthought.

The commander let himself in the front door.

*   *   *

'Something happened up at Green Willows.'

That remark stayed with me as I bade the commander good day and left the cottage.

'It was a long time ago.'

I thought of Green Willows—aloof, splendid—of the servants who would not live there, and of Mrs. Duffy's loneliness. I thought of Mr. Tremayne, as aloof as the house, isolated from others. I remembered the way people had acted when they had learned where I was going.

What had happened at Green Willows in that long-ago time that had left its mark on the place and on the people there?

I was so absorbed in these reflections that I was unaware that someone had spoken to me until she called to me again and stepped out from her doorway.

'Miss,' she said.

I stopped, turning to meet her. No doubt the questions in my mind must have left an impression on my face, for when I faced her, the woman stopped, almost startled.

'I'm sorry,' I said, laughing at myself and letting some of the tension drop away from me. 'I'm afraid I was lost in my thoughts.'

'And not very pleasant ones, I'd say,' She eyed me with frank curiosity. But she came the rest of the way to where I was waiting. She had come from the door of the local pub, I saw, and her apron and plain dress indicated that she worked there.

'I'm Mrs. Jenkins,' she introduced herself. 'I run the Duck and the Dog here since my husband died.'

'I'm Mary Kirkpatrick,' I said. 'I'm the new governess from Green Willows.'

'Oh, I know who you are,' she said, her head bobbing emphatically. She had a plain, open face, like a country field in summer, and her eyes, although grave now, could not entirely hide a warm light of friendliness.

There was an awkward pause, which I ended by saying, 'Can I do something for you, Mrs. Jenkins?'

She glanced down at her feet and then up at my face again. 'I was going to make up some excuse,' she said. 'Send something up to your housekeeper. But the truth is I only wanted to meet you.'

'I understand from Mrs. Duffy there's a great deal of curiosity about me,' I said with a smile. I rather liked her for that frank admission.

'Oh, them,' she said with a scornful gesture that seemed to include the entire village. 'A flock of geese. It's only, I think of that girl often, miss. I'm glad to know they've got someone to be with her, and now that I've met you, I'm glad it's someone young and pretty and pleasant.'

'Thank you, that's very kind, I'm sure,' I said, blushing a little. 'But this is my first job, and it remains to be seen how well I do. I'm rather on probation, I'm afraid.'

'Oh, aye, I've no doubt of that,' she said with an emphasis that I found hard to interpret. She leaned closer, lowering her voice as if sharing some secret with me. 'Just let me say, miss, if there's ever anything you need, or maybe just a place to come to get out of . . . well, if there's ever anything, you know where I am. Don't you hesitate to come to me.'

'Thank you,' I said. I did not know what else I could say, but she saved me the necessity of further remark.

'That's all I wanted to say,' she said, stepping back. 'Just remember it, and take good care of that little girl. She deserves it.'

'I shall,' I promised, and as she seemed to have finished, I nodded and added, 'Good day.' I went on, but when I glanced back a few yards along, she was still standing, watching me. I smiled and waved, and she nodded, but she did not wave back.

I nearly forgot to stop at the vicar's cottage to pick up Mrs. Duffy's eggs. Fortunately, I did remember when I saw the cottage, and I followed the little flower-lined path to the open door.

Isabelle Simpson, the vicar's sister, was a tall, spare-looking woman with very friendly brown eyes and a rough but ready personality. She was the sort of woman who probably could not cook worth a hang but did wonderful

59

things with her hands. I was pleased when my impression was somewhat confirmed; there was an easel in the parlor, where she had just been working on a watercolor.

'It's a hobby of mine,' she said, waving an apologetic hand at the easel, which rather occupied the room. 'Makes me feel that I'm doing *something*, if you know what I mean.'

'I think I do,' I said, accepting her offer of tea.

'Sorry my brother isn't here,' she said, leading the way into a diminutive and not-too-tidy kitchen. 'He rather wanted to meet you.'

'Along with everyone else,' I said. 'I am rather an object of curiosity, it seems.'

She laughed and said unashamedly, 'It's true. I was dying to get a look at you myself. Green Willows is an object of curiosity, you understand, and it's not every day someone new turns up there.'

The frank way in which she said this, though, had the immediate effect of dispelling some of the worrisome mists that had begun to cloud my thinking about my new home. In her bright kitchen, in the company of this no-nonsense woman, things seemed less mysterious and troubling.

'Green Willows is curious,' I agreed when she had poured the tea. We sat in the kitchen, which saved trying to talk around the easel. 'What did happen up there that makes everyone act so strangely toward the place?'

She frowned down at her teacup a moment. 'It's a long story,' she said, but not as if she were evading my question. 'Really, it should be saved for a longer visit. But it isn't anything that need affect you. I'd tell you if it should.'

'But it does seem to,' I said. 'People act so strange—and there's Elizabeth . . .'

'A charming girl, isn't she?' she said with a smile.

'Very—but to tell you the truth, she's unhappy. She wants to live at Green Willows. And I for one can't understand why she doesn't. It would seem the natural thing, wouldn't it?'

'Well, yes, but things aren't altogether natural at Green Willows, are they?'

I must have looked a bit alarmed at that because again she laughed and said, 'Oh, I didn't mean it like that. I suppose by now someone's told you the place is haunted or something like that?'

'No, that is, not exactly. But one can't help wondering . . . the way people act.'

'Green Willows has had a tragic history. Dark doings, violent deaths. Whenever that happens, people always begin to act strangely toward a house. Every wind in the eaves becomes someone moaning.'

This was so close to my own experience that I only nodded dumbly.

'And the personalities involved only encourage that sort of speculation. There's

Eleanor Tremayne, a cripple and a spinster—mind you, I'm a spinster too. But my situation is different, you see. My personality, my health, like a horse my brother says. My brother's position actually dictates that I mingle with people all the time, whereas she is an aloof person whose disability prevents her from going out and whose brother discourages anyone from coming in. And then there is Johnathon Tremayne himself. I suppose some would call him eccentric. At any rate, he is definitely antisocial. Under the circumstances, it was inevitable that people should begin to mutter about Green Willows. But I assure you, my dear, I have been there on several occasions, and I know of no dark deeds going on there that you need fear.'

'Then there is no reason why Elizabeth shouldn't come there to live?' I said.

'None, I'm quite sure. And I'm quite in agreement with you. I think it would be the best thing for her. Her grandfather is a fine man, and I've no doubt an excellent guardian. But Elizabeth is a young girl, sensitive, deprived of her mother. She needs a gentler hand too, a woman's touch. That's why I'm so glad you've come.'

She paused, then added, 'But I'm afraid you stand little chance of convincing either her father or her grandfather to let her come.'

'But why are they so against it if there's nothing wrong at Green Willows?'

She shrugged and said, 'I'm sure her father has his own reasons, which he's never confided to me. As for the grandfather, I expect he wants to keep his granddaughter away from her father just as he would have kept his daughter away from him if he could have. Oh, that's not to say there's anything wrong with Mr. Tremayne. I doubt that the commander would have approved of any man his daughter chose for a husband. The commander worshipped Angela—everyone did, it seems.'

'Didn't you?' I asked.

'I never knew her. I came after . . . after the troubles up there. But in all the years I've been here, I've never heard anyone describe her as else but an angel and a saint. Dear, you know, I love a good gossip, but Mrs. Duffy is expecting those eggs for lunch.'

'I hadn't realized it was so late,' I said, standing and finishing my tea. 'Thank you, it's been most enjoyable.'

'You must come again, drop in any time. We don't stand on much formality here, and it's good having someone to visit with.'

'I'm afraid I can't invite you to drop in,' I said. 'I don't know what privileges a governess has in that respect.'

'Never you mind,' she said.

I collected the eggs, pausing to admire some of her paintings that were hung on the walls. They had her boldness, but also her bright cheeriness. They suited the cottage well,

63

although I could not imagine them hanging at Green Willows.

At the door, though, a thought occurred to me. 'What did happen to Angela?' I asked.

She paused ever so slightly before she said, 'She was drowned in the lake in front of the house.'

I thought of the lake with the island and the little gazebo on it. No doubt that explained why they were so neglected. Perhaps it explained more. Johnathon Tremayne might be afraid that a similar accident would take his daughter from him. Maybe that was why, however illogically, he kept his daughter from the place.

'It was some sort of accident, I suppose,' I said.

Again that barely perceptible pause. 'As far as I know, there's no one alive who knows,' she said.

I began to understand even more. 'And that,' I said, 'is why some people are so afraid of Green Willows. Some of them must say . . . there must be rumors that her death was . . . not an accident.'

'Some of them do say that,' she said.

CHAPTER SEVEN

Isabelle Simpson's blunt, level-headed appraisal of the situation did much to alleviate my fears. And yet while I could logically agree with what she said, and even laugh at the idea that something might be really wrong with the house, the fears remained, thrust down into my subconscious mind, but only just below the surface, waiting to come forth at the slightest provocation. And there were provocations.

I recall that same day, walking home from the vicar's cottage, I took the path that led over the hill and around the birches. As I came in sight of the lake with its little island, I slowed my steps and finally, on an impulse, crossed the arched bridge to the island and again stood in the gazebo.

My eyes searched the green surface of the lake as if I might see tiny bubbles of air rising, but the water was as still and smooth as glass.

A woman had drowned here. The gazebo had been witness to her final struggles. The finches that nested in its cornice had heard her cries and perhaps had gaily called back to her.

Or had there been another witness, someone who heard her cries and failed to come to her aid?

Something snapped behind me, and a shadow fell across the stone floor. I started and whirled about for all the world as if I expected someone to try to drown me.

'I'm sorry, did I startle you?' Johnathon Tremayne asked.

'I . . . I was thinking about something,' I stammered, embarrassed at my own skittishness.

His eyes went to the water's surface as if he had read my thoughts. But he only said, 'I saw you come across, and I thought I ought to warn you. This place is pretty neglected. I wouldn't want the roof collapsing on you.'

I nearly glanced up but caught myself in time. The roof, I was sure, was quite solid, despite the obvious neglect.

'It's a lovely place, though,' I said.

He looked around at the gazebo itself, at the little stone bench, at the weeds slowly covering everything.

'Yes,' he said. 'My wife designed all this.'

The irony of that struck me—she had designed the place of her own death. I felt that I must say something, and I rather blurted out, 'You must have loved her very much.'

'She was a saint,' he said, but with such a peculiar vehemence that I must have looked actually surprised, for he smiled faintly and said, 'Indeed, everyone says so, and it's true, she was very saintlike.'

I found myself thinking that I was not sure I would want to live with an actual saint, although I was prepared to admit that the fault

66

was in my own gross inadequacies of saintliness. I wondered how this man had coped with such magnificent goodness. He was a very earthbound man, I thought, no angel he. I was conscious, in this quiet, secluded spot, of an earthy masculinity about him; far from being frightened of him, as I had expected to be, I felt myself oddly drawn toward him. I saw that it was hurt and loneliness and an inability to share those feelings with others that cut him off from his fellow man, that made him seem gruff and cold. I had a most singular urge to reach out to him, to touch him simply, to comfort him, although I could imagine with some amusement how he would react to that.

The silence between us lasted for some minutes, but it was not at all awkward. He seemed to feel no need to fill up each minute with talk, and I found myself quite content merely to be here as we were, to let him think his thoughts, and to bring his attention back to me when he was ready.

At last, he brought his gaze back to me and asked, 'How did the lessons go?'

'Very well,' I said. 'Your daughter is quite bright, and I think you'll be amazed at how quickly she progresses.'

'Good,' he said, nodding. And after a minute, he added, 'It would help in certain quarters, you understand, if you were able to show proof of your success. Her grandfather, as you may have realized, is not altogether convinced of the wisdom of hiring you.'

'I got that impression,' I said drily.

He half smiled at me. 'I'm afraid I've brought you into a difficult situation without giving you a full understanding in advance of what it would entail. And in all honesty, it may get even more difficult as time goes by. Under the circumstances, I would not consider it unreasonable if you asked to be freed from our contract.'

'That won't be necessary,' I said, and I fancy he looked pleased. But he looked less pleased at my next remark. 'There is one thing, though, that I feel rather strongly about and that I wish to discuss with you further.'

He sighed and said, 'Is it about bringing my daughter back to Green Willows?' I nodded. 'I thought as much,' he said. 'I didn't fancy that once you got that idea in your head you would let go of it easily.'

I started to say something, but he made a gesture of silence and, taking my hand, led me to the bench, where he sat beside me.

'Surely, in the brief time you have spent with her,' he said, 'you have seen that my daughter is obsessed with the memory of her mother?'

'I believe that keeping her completely away from Green Willows only fires that obsession,' I said. 'It is quite natural for a girl to miss her mother, to want to see her mother's things, to be where her mother was. I know because I have experienced a similar loss. If you will not permit your daughter a normal outlet for these longings, you deny her the release she needs for her grief in order to adjust to it.'

His lips remained their usual stern line, but I thought I saw a glint of amusement in his eyes as he said, 'And do you think that you can persuade her grandfather to agree to your way of thinking?'

'I had rather hoped you would do that,' I said frankly. This time he truly did smile.

'Yes,' he said, as if concluding some private conversation of his own. 'A very remarkable girl.'

He had taken my hand when he led me to the bench, and he still held it in his own rough one. I saw that he was looking down, studying my hand. Mine are not very pretty hands; I have had to work all my life. I fancied that in his mind's eyes he was comparing my hand to his wife's lovely ones, and oddly, I found that I resented the comparison. I took my hand from his. He did not try to prevent my doing so.

'Miss Kirkpatrick,' he said, and his voice had suddenly gone sterner. 'I agree with what you say, but I must point out that you have only been here briefly. There are things you know nothing about.'

'There is a simple solution to that,' I said. 'You have only to explain the additional circumstances to me.'

He stared at me for so long that I thought

he was thinking how best to rebuke me for what even I had to admit was a blatant effrontry. I, who was only a governess and a new one in the bargain, certainly had no business asking my employer to explain anything to me.

All he did, though, was to stand quite abruptly and say, 'I will consider this further. And now, I think Mrs. Duffy is expecting those eggs, and no doubt you will be glad for some lunch.'

I stood too. I cannot think what boldness prompted me to ask, 'Will you be having lunch also?'

He looked actually startled by the question. I suppose people did not ordinarily question him about anything. His gruff manner should have discouraged me as well, except that I thought it largely a bluff.

'I usually eat alone,' he said. His tone did not encourage further remarks from me, and I allowed him to escort me over the bridge and back to Green Willows.

But when lunch was served, he was seated at his place at the head of the table.

*　　　*　　　*

I found that he went often to the little island. Time after time, I saw him strolling the island's diminutive shoreline or seated in the gazebo, lost in thought. I did not want to intrude upon his solitude unduly; I thought, or at least hoped, that he was considering my request, and I thought it best to bide my time.

With each passing day, the newness of my place at Green Willows and of Green Willows itself wore off. I cannot say that I ever came to feel comfortable there; there was a strange lurking sense of fear that I could not, or would not, put into words. For a time, though, nothing untoward happened.

I pursued my studies with Elizabeth, and her progress was truly remarkable. She and I seemed to have established an immediate closeness that made our mornings together quite enjoyable. Although she talked about her mother, she did not again pursue the subject of her return to Green Willows, only, I think, because she trusted that I was doing all that I could do.

It was difficult to say what impression I was making on the commander. He continued to leave each morning when I arrived and to return at my appointed time of departure. Only once did he offer any personal comment, and then it was not about my teaching but about what I suppose would be classified as my social life.

As I was clearly an object of curiosity to the local people, I was quickly acquainted with many of the townswomen. I could not say that I was friends with them; in this corner of England, an outsider could live here a lifetime and still remain an outsider. But they talked to me willingly enough, and I soon knew many of them by name.

Whether by chance or by design, I saw Mrs. Jenkins every day. Sometimes she was at the door of her pub, and she never failed to greet me and to eye me with that strange air of wary speculation. At other times, I passed her in the street, and we stopped to make conversation. She never asked anything directly about Elizabeth or about affairs at Green Willows, and the only information I volunteered was in reference to Elizabeth's progress at her studies. I could not help but wonder exactly what her interest in Elizabeth was, but I was certain that hers was something more than idle curiosity.

It was these brief, seemingly inconsequential meetings with Mrs. Jenkins that provoked the commander to break his silence with me. He was at his window one day when I chanced to encounter Mrs. Jenkins and to exchange remarks upon the weather. I thought nothing of his watchful presence, and his look was no more disapproving than usual. Nevertheless, I had hardly begun the morning lessons when he appeared at the doorway and asked to speak to me alone.

'I do not regard the proprietress of a tavern as a suitable companion for my granddaughter,' he said in a chilling voice. 'Nor for my granddaughter's governess.'

'I would not have described Mrs. Jenkins and myself as companions,' I said, for once maintaining my composure, although I was furious at what I considered unwarranted snobbery. 'We have hardly more than spoken to each other.'

'In the street,' he pointed out. 'And the Lord alone knows where else. In the future, if you are to have a future here, you will kindly conduct yourself with more discretion.'

He did not wait to hear what I might say further—indeed, I was so furious that it was unlikely any words would have come, and had they done so, it was as well he was not there to hear them.

But when I returned to Elizabeth and had calmed down somewhat, I reasoned that I would have to be circumspect for the girl's sake. To antagonize the commander now would not only result in my dismissal but would certainly dash any hopes of a governess for her or for her return to Green Willows.

Fortunately, I was not forced to an awkward decision, as for some time after that I only saw Mrs. Jenkins at the door of her pub. I was careful to give a friendly greeting but to pass without slowing my steps. Perhaps she understood what the problem was, as she did not try to detain me.

*   *   *

73

I paid several visits to Isabelle Simpson, and from her and from a certain Miss Meriweather, who was the only other local to invite me to tea, I gradually pieced together a story of past events at Green Willows, a story that both cleared up questions and raised new ones.

Johnathon Tremayne was the son of a local man who had made himself a tidy sum in shipbuilding, among other interests, which Johnathon gradually took over for his father. The commander was a local man who had lived abroad for many years, where his daughter was born. Upon the death of his wife, the commander retired and brought his daughter back to their cottage.

In almost no time, Johnathon and Angela had met and had fallen in love. The commander railed and resisted, but love would have its way, and the two young people were married. Johnathon built Green Willows for his bride, and they went there to live.

To the villagers, Angela was indeed like an angel. 'She was an outsider, you see,' Isabelle explained. 'But she was so very beautiful— you'll have seen the portrait of her at the house?'

'Yes. She was lovely, wasn't she,' I said.

'It doesn't begin to do her justice,' Miss Meriweather had told me. 'When you first saw her, she almost took your breath away.'

'But it was more than just the way she

looked. She was so good, so wonderful. Everyone who knew her talked of her piety. She went to church regularly, she was generous to the poor, and she spoke always in the same sweet, soft voice, never losing her temper, never raising her voice, or never in any way being short with anyone. You couldn't annoy her; you couldn't offend her. She was in every way a paragon of virtue.'

'She sounds too good to be true,' I said.

'I would have said so myself,' Isabelle agreed. 'But everyone I've talked to says the same things about her.'

'If the Virgin Mary were to come down to earth,' Miss Meriweather put it, 'she wouldn't hold a candle to what Miss Angela was.'

'It was an idyllic situation,' Isabelle said. 'The beautiful, virtuous mistress of that beautiful house, her hard-driving, successful husband . . . the happy ending to a romantic story. But it wasn't the ending, you see; it was only the beginning.'

'And when the end came, it wasn't a happy one,' I suggested.

She nodded and said, 'Exactly.'

She paused to pour some more tea before going on. I accepted mine politely, although I was far more interested in hearing the rest of the story.

'Angela took sick,' she said, settling back in her chair. 'From what I gather, she was never particularly strong. At any rate, she was abed for a time, and after that, she went abroad. Johnathon was deeply involved in business and the new estate and wasn't able to leave just then, so she went with her nurse and constant companion, Mrs. Woodridge. She is one of the more interesting persons in the story.'

'Miss Meriweather talked of her as some sort of dragon,' I said.

'I suppose she was. Angela was so nice, you know, so agreeable, there would had to have been someone to say no, someone to be stern. From all I've heard, Mrs. Woodridge was just the ticket. She was devoted to Angela, never left her side if she could help it, and there was nothing she wouldn't do for her. I don't know, of course, but they say she didn't hesitate for a minute to give Johnathon how-do-you-do if she thought he was not treating his wife properly.'

'That must have made for an interesting domestic scene,' I said. I found it difficult to imagine anyone giving Johnathon Tremayne how-do-you-do; Mrs. Woodridge must indeed have been fearless.

'One does wonder,' Isabelle said. 'Of course, as I've said, I wasn't here. Angela would have needed someone to be firm, and it's logical others would have resented Mrs. Woodridge if she tried to stand between them and Angela. It's hard to know what the real story was.'

She paused. She had been looking past me

at a watercolor on the easel. 'I wish you'd tell me,' she said, 'if that blue in the sky is right or wrong. I've been looking at it while we talked, and it looks all wrong to me.'

Just then I could not have cared if the sky were polka dot, but I turned obligingly and gave my opinion that the sky in the painting looked entirely natural to me.

'But I hasten to add, I'm no judge of art,' I said.

'I wish I could go to Italy. They say it gives your work an entirely different perspective,' she said, irrelevantly, I thought, until she added, 'That was where they went, to Italy.'

I was glad we were back to her story and relaxed gratefully into my chair again.

'They were gone more than a year,' she went on. 'And when they returned, they were not two, but four. In that time Angela had discovered that she was pregnant and had remained to have the child there.'

'He didn't join her when he learned of her condition?'

'No.' She shrugged. 'It's hard to say why. Perhaps she preferred that he didn't. Husbands can be nuisances in those situations, and I suspect from all that I've heard that Mrs. Woodridge wouldn't have wanted him around under those circumstances. In addition to which, Johnathon's father died, which kept him here.'

'They came back four, you said.'

'Yes,' she said, smiling. 'And this is where things become really interesting. They brought back an Italian girl; her name was Gina. A full-blown peasant type. Le Baux has painted the sort a hundred times, if you're familiar with his canvasses. She was lovely to look at, and she spoke no more than a few words of English. Angela had adopted her.'

'Adopted her? What on earth for?' I asked.

'Only in a manner of speaking. The girl was Angela's ward, and from this rough stock, she intended to mold, as she put it, another angel.'

'And did she succeed,' I asked. I, who had found the thought of living with even one angel difficult, positively shrank away from the prospect of two.

'The troubles Gina brought with her were anything but angelic, if one can credit the stories. For one thing, she was simply not welcomed into the community.'

'A foreigner,' Miss Meriweather would describe her, 'with her damned foreign ways. Nobody liked her. Couldn't even talk to her; she always talked foreign.'

'And for another,' Isabelle explained, 'it was blatantly transparent from the first day she arrived that she was smitten with her handsome new master. Perhaps it would only have provided some local gossip and a few laughs if Angela and Johnathon hadn't been the romantic idyll of the community, and Angela hadn't been so literally worshipped here. But no one was going to tolerate a foreigner's encroachment, however innocent.'

'And was it innocent?' I asked. I had, when this part of the story was related to me, had a strange experience. I suddenly thought that I could understand, even sympathize, with this Italian girl's infatuation with Johnathon Tremayne. I had not thought of him in that way before, and yet there it was—he was older now, but more than years had etched his face with deep lines and shadows. He was not handsome, I would say, but from the first, I had experienced some unfamiliar attraction to him. And Gina had been in a strange place, among strangers, unable even to speak the language.

And with angels, yet. How difficult it must have been for her, with the perfect Angela and the stern Mrs. Woodridge. But Johnathon— earthy, real, gruff perhaps but capable of gentleness—he was there too, and who could wonder that a lonely girl's heart had gone out to him?

'Who can say, really?' Isabelle said, shrugging her slim shoulders. 'There were rumors of all sorts. Some say that Johnathon was obviously troubled during this time, that he became daily more moody and withdrawn. Of course, they would say it was because he had fallen in love with Gina.'

'I would have thought the obvious solution would have been simply to send the girl back to Italy,' I said.

'That would have been admitting defeat, for one thing. And who knows, maybe Angela knew that there was nothing to it. I do know that everyone says that where another wife might have railed and quarreled Angela was only that much sweeter to the girl.

'Exactly what happened from there on is only conjecture. No one in the village was actually in the house at the time, and they could only say what they observed from the outside, as it were. Gina became more and more troublesome, the master more and more withdrawn. Inevitably, things built up to a tragic climax. Some sort of quarrel erupted— you can guess what people say it was about. Angela was drowned in the lake.'

'And people say Gina murdered her.'

'Many people have said so, but I doubt that the truth will ever be known. There was a violent storm that night. It is entirely likely, even probable, that Angela somehow fell into the lake and drowned. In any event, Gina ran away that same night. She was found hiding in a ditch a few days later and was brought back to Green Willows, but she was suffering from pneumonia and unable to tell anyone anything about what happened. She died soon after without ever giving her side of the story.'

'Both dead,' I murmured. 'Within a few days of each other.'

'Yes. Mrs. Woodridge left, of course. I

understand that she lives in Brighton now, and Johnathon Tremayne withdrew from the world. He sold out his business interests and cut off his ties with the outside world. His sister came to live with him. And the stories began to grow up around them and around Green Willows.'

'I suppose this explains too the coldness between Mr. Tremayne and the commander.'

'Yes,' Isabelle said. 'The commander never ceased to blame Johnathon for his daughter's death. For a time, Johnathon kept the baby with him, but eventually, he gave in to the commander or perhaps he really didn't want her there. Perhaps she was too much of a reminder. Anyway, Elizabeth was sent to live with her grandfather.'

'You know,' I said thoughtfully, 'until now we've talked about what it means to Elizabeth to be shut away from Green Willows and from the memories of her mother. But I think perhaps that her father is also being deprived by this separation, deprived of the love he needs to help him recover from this tragedy. Surely, a daughter's love would do a great deal to free him from the past.'

'I believe Johnathon is in great need of love,' Isabelle said, collecting the tea things. She gave me a peculiar look that I could not interpret, but her brother arrived home just then, and our conversation turned to other subjects. The vicar did not approve of his sister's gossiping.

CHAPTER EIGHT

It was on the day following this conversation that I received a surprise when I went for Elizabeth's lessons. I thought that the commander looked even more grim-faced than usual, and I saw at once that Elizabeth was on a high plane of barely contained excitement.

He had no sooner gone than she burst out, 'I'm coming to dinner at Green Willows.'

I confess our lessons were rather loose that day, although we both made the effort; our thoughts would not stray far from the coming evening. Elizabeth could offer no enlightenment regarding the circumstances of the invitation, only that her grandfather had told her, shortly before I arrived, that she would be going there this same evening for dinner.

Of one thing I was certain—it had not been the commander's idea, and however his compliance had been obtained, it had been given grudgingly. I had actually toyed with the idea of mentioning the subject to him, to see if I could learn more, but one glimpse of his icy visage removed that temptation, and I returned to Green Willows unenlightened.

I was not so frightened of Johnathon

Tremayne, though, and when I saw him in the gazebo, I hesitated only a moment before crossing the bridge to join him; he saw my approach and regarded me without expression until I had reached his side.

'You've heard?' he asked.

'Yes,' I said, finding myself suddenly speechless.

'And are you not pleased?' His voice had an irritated ring to it that only added to my unexpected self-consciousness.

'Of course, but that's hardly the point, is it?' I said. 'It wasn't to please me, after all.'

There was only the faintest of pauses before he said, 'Of course not.' He took my arm as if he would escort me back across the bridge.

Made bold by the gesture, I said, 'Have you spoken to her grandfather about . . .'

'I have spoken to her grandfather about her coming here tonight for dinner,' he said. 'Before a child can walk, he must take that first step. As a teacher, you should know that, Miss Kirkpatrick. Be content with the first step.'

He had spoken quite sharply, but now, much more gently, he added, 'Please.'

I let him lead me back to the house.

*　　　*　　　*

I cannot describe that dinner as anything but awkward. To begin with, Eleanor Tremayne was in some sort of pique. She hardly spoke at all, and when she did, it was in a curt manner.

The master was not loquacious at the best of times, and to make things worse, he sat at the head of the table with the air of a man weighing and making decisions.

That this communicated itself to Elizabeth was inevitable, and her natural youthful uncertainty was only made worse.

All in all, I do not think she acquitted herself badly. She only dropped a spoon on the floor, which, I believed, was overshadowed by my tipping over a wineglass. She had a tendency to chatter, nervousness causing her to want to fill up all those vast empty spaces, and I did my best to respond and even tried without avail to include her father and aunt in the conversation.

I was grateful when the meal was ended. Ordinarily, I retired to my room after a meal; Eleanor and I were not in the habit of withdrawing together, but I did not know what the right form would be for this occasion.

As if sensing my indecision, Johnathon spoke to me directly for the first time that evening, suggesting that I take Elizabeth to the drawing room.

'You must excuse me,' Eleanor said, wheeling her chair about sharply. 'But I have a headache. I'll go to my own room as usual.'

I saw the hurt look that fluttered across Elizabeth's face, and I knew that she was immediately assessing herself, asking what she had done wrong to turn her aunt against her.

It was presumptuous of me, but my success with a 'first step' prompted me to boldness. When we had retired, I left Elizabeth alone and went to Eleanor's room. She met me at the door, and her manner was so unwelcoming that I supposed she knew why I had come. Nonetheless, I persisted.

I asked after her headache, and she told me it was much the same. Then I said, 'It's so rarely your niece comes for a visit, and I know she would be thrilled if you could manage to spend even a few minutes with us.'

'No doubt she would,' Eleanor said. 'But I was opposed to this visit, as I am opposed to your scheme to move Elizabeth back to Green Willows. You shall not have your way in this, I promise you. I won't have Elizabeth living here.'

'But why?' I asked, so astonished at this vehement outburst that I forgot my position entirely. 'What can you have against it?'

'That, Miss Kirkpatrick, is my business and not yours,' she said, and with that, she shut the door almost on my nose.

I returned downstairs in a deeply chastened mood. If Eleanor Tremayne was opposed to moving Elizabeth back to Green Willows, it was hardly likely that my opinion would prevail. What was worse, I could think of no logical reason for her position. Nothing in the tragic story that I had heard about Green Willows had indicated that she played any part in it; as far as I knew, she had come to live with her brother after the death of his wife. It was another mystery with which the house seemed crowded.

At least Elizabeth did not seem to be minding her aunt's absence. As I neared the drawing room, I heard her humming; it was the same little song I had heard her humming before; the one she told me her mother used to hum. For a fleeting moment, it reminded me of her mother's locked room upstairs. But I did not want to consider that because I did not yet know what I thought about it. I thrust it aside and came into the room.

As I did so, I noticed what I had not before: Elizabeth was wearing perfume. The room was filled with the scent of gardenias, so much so that I thought that in the future I should caution her about applying her scent a bit more judiciously. For now, though, I thought she had had enough criticism, if only implied, and I settled for going to the french windows and opening them slightly to admit a fresh breeze.

It was not until I turned from the windows that I actually observed Elizabeth. When I did so, I felt a quick pang of anxiety. She again had that dangerous-looking air of barely contained excitement. Her face was flushed, and her eyes had an almost feverish quality.

My first thought was that the evening's excitement had been a bit too much for her, and I went quickly to her. 'Perhaps you ought to come over here in the air,' I said, putting an arm about her shoulders.

'Oh, Mary,' she said, hugging me delightedly. 'Thank you, thank you so much for bringing me here.'

'You're welcome, I'm sure,' I said. 'But I think your gratitude is misplaced. It was your father who arranged this evening, and I think you should find an opportunity to thank him properly. I know it would make him . . .'

She did not let me finish; indeed, I hardly think she heard a word I said. She said, 'She's here.'

At first, I did not understand, and thinking Eleanor had repented and had come down to join us, I looked toward the hall, but there was no one there.

'Who is here?' I asked.

Elizabeth broke away from me as if she could not bear to stand still a minute longer. She threw her head back and gave a girlish laugh and did a little dance turn about the room, again humming to herself.

I felt a pang of alarm; I had never seen her quite so worked up and could not imagine that even this unaccustomed visit could have so much effect.

'Elizabeth,' I said. 'Come and sit down with me over here. You look utterly beside yourself.'

'I am,' she said, but she came obediently to my outstretched hand and let me lead her to a little divan near the windows.

'Now,' I said. 'Calmly, please. What did you mean? Who is here?'

'My mother,' she said, laughing again almost hysterically. 'She came to see me, just now, before you came down.'

CHAPTER NINE

I no longer recall what I said to Elizabeth that evening or even exactly what I said to myself. I made myself a reasonable-sounding explanation. Elizabeth was highly excited and had been under a considerable strain throughout the evening. She was in the place that she had so passionately longed to be, and although she had been only an infant when she had been here, it was plausible that each room still triggered heretofore forgotten memories. Under the circumstances, it was not really remarkable that she should think she saw her mother.

But I did not test these explanations on anyone else, and I cautioned Elizabeth to say nothing of her 'experience' to anyone. I think I promised myself I would take it up as soon as possible with Isabelle Simpson—she with her cool head and her logic for everything. But I never once contemplated saying anything to Johnathon Tremayne.

Later in the evening, just before we were to take Elizabeth back to her grandfather's cottage, she found her way to the stairs, and I found her seated before her mother's portrait, staring soulfully up at it. I snatched her away a bit angrily, but not before I too stared upward into that painted face. It seemed to me as if those angelic eyes regarded me with faint mockery, and when at the end of the evening I retired to my room, I passed the portrait with my eyes carefully turned away.

*   *   *

In the morning, though, I was less dismayed by the incident, and in the light of day I was more inclined to accept my own explanations for it. In any event, I did not discuss it with Isabelle Simpson, as planned, because subsequent events of greater moment distracted me.

I had just come down for breakfast when Johnathon told me that I need not go to the cottage this day.

'Shouldn't I inform the commander?' I asked, surprised by this turn of events.

'That won't be necessary. I'll be seeing him myself,' Johnathon said. 'And I'll take all the blame, never fear.'

89

'I wasn't afraid,' I said, and indeed, I was much too curious to be afraid, but for once, I kept my questions to myself. I saw Johnathon go out, his cloak billowing in the wind, as he rode toward town. I was left to pace the downstairs rooms and wonder. Eleanor was still in her room, and I reflected that perhaps I had done her an injustice in assuming her headache was nothing more than pique. I would have visited her in her room and inquired after her health, but our last meeting had been so negative that I was not at all sure she would welcome seeing me, although I for one would have been glad for someone to talk to other than Mrs. Duffy, who was preoccupied and not very conversational.

Afterward, Elizabeth informed me that it had been a singularly stormy meeting between her father and grandfather, even for those two fiery individuals. She could not tell me much of what was said, for, although their voices were raised, the specific words did not carry to the parlor, where she waited the outcome of the meeting.

The outcome was that her father again had his way, and Elizabeth moved to Green Willows.

When I first heard the news, I was inclined, a trifle foolishly perhaps, to think of it as my little triumph, just as later I was to consider it largely my fault, which is only a different way of saying the same thing. Later, though, I had much to blame myself for, and if I had known how tragedy would follow my actions, as a hunter stalks his wounded prey, I would surely have taken a different course.

I did not learn of this turn of events until evening, for, although Johnathon was back late that morning, he did not confide in me. I saw him on his little island, but he looked so preoccupied, in fact so angry, that I did not venture to approach him but instead stayed timidly in my room most of the afternoon. So much for the spunk with which the commander had credited me.

At dinner, Johnathon informed us, Eleanor and me, of the news. My reaction was instinctive.

'Oh, how wonderful,' I cried, throwing decorum to the wind and delightedly clapping my hands like a little girl at Christmas.

My enthusiasm was short-lived, however; I had forgotten Eleanor's objections to such a scheme, but she was quick to remind us of them.

'Wonderful?' she said in a voice that was the more dampening for being so small and quiet. 'Johnathon, you can't be serious in this. I forbid you to move that girl into this house.'

While I am quick to admit that presumption is one of my faults, I would hever have been so bold as to speak to a man like Johnathon Tremayne in that way, and my reaction was literally to shrink back into my chair. Later, I reflected that Johnathon had not forgotten Eleanor's objections, had in fact been dreading them. I think that he had already experienced some guilt in presenting her, as it were, with an accomplished fact, and this was perhaps why he reacted so angrily to her words.

'You will not forbid me, Eleanor,' he said, his voice as quiet and as chilling as hers had been. 'It is already done. Elizabeth will be here tomorrow.'

There was a long moment of silence. I looked from one to the other, but neither of them had a glance for me. Their eyes were locked together, and I was conscious of some quarrel going on on a silent level, something of which I knew nothing and in which I had no voice. They knew something, those two, of Green Willows, of Elizabeth's return, that I did not know, but even then, I had a momentary pang of doubt—had I done the right thing in pushing for this?

Eleanor left the dining room without another word, the soft whirring of the wheels of her chair like a punctuation mark emphasizing her disapproval. Had I known what was before us, I would surely not have sat silently as I did, watching the stiff set of her shoulders, the angry line of her mouth.

Eleanor. Had I only been kinder. Had I only tried to talk of it with you. To say that was not my place is no excuse. I had already so overstepped my place that one more foray could not have mattered, and it could have saved so much.

It was an embarrassing moment when she had gone, for, although I had instigated this move, had encouraged it, I was still an employee who had witnessed a disagreement between my employer and his relative. I would have followed Eleanor's example; indeed, had risen to do so, but Johnathon waved me back into my chair with an angry gesture that I dared not ignore. He too had risen as Eleanor left, but now he sat back down again and poured himself a glass of wine from the blown-glass decanter that sat before him. For a moment, he sat staring moodily into its ruby depths.

With a quick movement, he lifted the glass, drained it, and set it down again with a bang. 'She'll get used to it,' he said, pushing his chair back noisily. He too left, leaving me alone in the dining room, dinner only half concluded.

Elizabeth moved back to Green Willows in the morning. I did not see the commander, whose reaction to the move must have been no more approving than Eleanor's. I did not see her either, and Johnathon, whom I did see, was in an angry mood so that the occasion could hardly have been described as a jubilant one.

Elizabeth was well trained, though, in restraining her feelings and knew how the wind blew. I, in fact, took my cue from her and guarded my feelings carefully until we were alone. Once in her room—the little nursery downstairs had been converted into an attractive room for a girl, with a little study-desk and chintz curtains—we hugged each other and soon made a party out of the occasion. Mrs. Duffy was cautiously pleased and brought us some hot chocolate and some cookies that Cook had made especially in honor of the new resident.

'I can hardly believe I'm really here,' Elizabeth cried, stuffing an entire cookie into her mouth and managing somehow to laugh at the same time.

'There, this house could use some laughter,' Mrs. Duffy said, quickly adding, 'Not that I've been unhappy here, mind, but there's nothing like young people to brighten a place.'

I confess that lessons that day were a haphazard affair; I had to set my mind to them, and Elizabeth did so poorly that I was shocked into a more sober frame of mind. I had not the slightest doubt that a lapse in her progress would soon provoke a move back to the commander's cottage. I warned her of this in the strongest terms, so she did finally buckle down. Still, the atmosphere in the little schoolroom remained a festive one, except for one thing.

'I'm afraid we've picked the coldest room in the house for our lessons,' I said, rubbing my arms to try to offset the chill, which was becoming more uncomfortable, it seemed, with each passing moment. The hired man had laid a fire, just in case, and although I had assured him at the time that it was not necessary, I now decided it should be lit. Even that however, did not dispel the damp chill that pervaded the room, so that in time it was necessary to abandon lessons altogether in favor of reading in my room, where the sun kept it comfortable most of the time without a fire.

I had wondered during the morning if Elizabeth and I would lunch alone, but when we came down, Johnathon was already at his place. Eleanor was conspicuously absent, and after seeing us seated, Johnathon excused himself and left the room. I heard his heavy tread on the stairs and anticipated another stormy meal if Eleanor were forced to lunch with us. Someone would have to give in; Elizabeth was of too sensitive and excitable a disposition to take too much friction without ill effects, and I made up my mind that when Johnathon was in a more receptive frame of mind I would ask him to let Elizabeth and me take our meals in the nursery for a while.

I heard him on the stairs; Eleanor used a ramp built at the rear of the main hall, but I did not hear her. When Johnathon came in, his expression was one of concern rather than anger.

'Have you seen Eleanor this morning?' he asked me, pausing in the doorway.

'No,' I said. 'Not since . . . not since dinner last evening.'

He glanced at Elizabeth, who shook her head.

'Nor have I,' he said. He crossed the dining room with rapid strides and disappeared in the direction of the kitchen, but when he came back from there, his look was no more enlightened that before.

'Please,' he said to the two of us, 'eat your lunch. I'll manage something later.'

We did as he bade us, and Elizabeth's youthful appetite allowed her to do justice to Cook's delicious food, but I only picked at mine. I had begun to feel the weight of some impending tragedy; it was as if my nerve endings were all reaching out, straining toward something that my conscious mind could not yet distinguish. There was no reason to suspect disaster, and yet even while I picked at my fish, I was preparing myself for it.

Green Willows was a large house, and a thorough search of it took some hours. I do not know what anyone thought; I told myself half-heartedly that Eleanor was in another of her moods and had simply found some corner of the house in which to hide herself. I myself liked to withdraw from others when I was angry or unhappy and had often taken myself up to a little-used corner of the attic at

Mrs. White's. No doubt, I reasoned, Eleanor had some such place of her own here, and that was where she would eventually be found.

Yet as the day wore on, my conviction in that theory grew steadily weaker. I could suppose that Eleanor might leave her dinner untouched and spend the evening locked in her room. I could suppose that in the morning she might disregard breakfast and hide herself away in some private corner to be alone. And she might stay away from lunch. But it was now late afternoon. More than twenty-four hours had gone by since, as far as we knew, she had eaten and almost that long since anyone had seen her. Either she was greatly overdoing the urge for solitude or something was amiss.

The afternoon was intended to be more or less free for Elizabeth and me, but neither of us had shown any inclination to go off alone, and so we had stayed together. I took her for a stroll down to the lake, where we explored the little island, and I informed her that it had been done to her mother's design.

'Let's fix it up,' she said, brushing some cobwebs from a pilaster. 'It could be so beautiful.'

I had to agree that it could, but as I looked around, trying to see it through her eyes, I felt a pang. This in my mind was Johnathon's retreat. I had gotten used to seeing him here alone, pondering his private thoughts as he gazed at the water's surface.

'I must ask your father,' I said. 'But not today. Anyway, there's much that we couldn't do—I don't know how sound this place is, for one thing. I expect we'd have to have men in.'

'But we could do the cleaning,' she cried. 'We could put on aprons and borrow dusters from Mrs. Duffy. It would be fun, wouldn't it?'

'Perhaps,' I said, noncommittally. In my mind's eye, I was seeing the commander's reaction to seeing his granddaughter turned into a cleaning lady, complete with apron and duster. I thought he would be less than enthusiastic, but I kept this thought to myself.

At Elizabeth's insistence, we walked to the cliff that overlooked the sea. I did not often come here, and although my room overlooked this side of the house, I did not care for the view. The solitary wind-gnarled tree seemed like a warning sentry, reminding one of the dangers of that downhill slope that led to the cliff's edge and to the sheer drop to the waves and rocks below.

I wondered how Angela Tremayne had felt about this rugged vista. Surely, the lake with its graceful willows and its elegant gazebo must have better reflected her tastes. That, no doubt, was why the house had turned its back upon the cliff and why she had designed that soothing pastoral scene in front.

It had rained lightly the night before, and even at the driest of times, the sea mist and breeze kept things damp on this side of the house. We found it necessary to lift our skirts a little to keep them from getting wet in the long grass.

Had it not been for this, I would probably have never noticed the furrows in the ground where the grass had been crushed down. At first, I did not grasp the significance, and even when I had decided that they were tracks made by some wheeled vehicle, I still did not immediately experience any alarm.

It was the handkerchief that seemed suddenly to jar everything into focus. Elizabeth saw it first, a bit of cambric almost lost in the grass.

'Look,' she cried, seizing it up. 'It's Aunt Eleanor's.'

'So it is,' I said, taking it from her. A neat 'E T' had been embroidered in one corner.

I looked down at the spot where it had been lying and then at the twin furrows in the ground, and suddenly, I saw them for what they were—tracks left by her wheelchair.

I felt as if icy fingers suddenly grabbed my heart, and I think I gasped. I followed the line of the tracks; they could be seen clearly, leading down the slope, down past the crooked tree, down . . . all the way to the cliff's edge.

'Elizabeth, wait here, please,' I said in as even a voice as I could manage.

'Why?' she asked innocently. 'What is . . . ?'

'Just wait here,' I said firmly. I did not wait for arguments but left her and began to walk toward the cliff's edge, following the trail of those grooves.

I did not like approaching that edge. The wind seemed suddenly to leap up, a living thing clutching at me, at my gown and my hair. In my imagination, it seemed to be trying to urge me on, to seize me and pull me faster and faster, forward and down. It was like a whispering voice, coaxing me to hurry, to run, run, run.

I stopped several feet back from the edge. There was an overhang, and from here, I could see nothing of the shore below, only the white-crowned waves rushing in toward it. For some reason, I could not bring myself to go any closer, and while I cursed myself for a coward, still some instinct held me back. At last, I hurried back to Elizabeth.

'What's happened?' she asked. 'You look dreadful.'

'I'll explain later,' I said, taking her hand and practically jerking her around. 'Come, we've got to find your father.'

Once in the house, I sent Elizabeth, over her objections, to her room and sought Johnathon. He was out, having gone into town to make inquiries about his sister. I waited for him, and when I heard the sound of horse's hooves approaching, I went to meet him. When I told him what I had found, his face went ashen, and he rushed around the house to see for himself.

Farther along the headland, a precipitous path made a portion of the beach accessible for bathing, but here the only way down was by rope. The rest of that afternoon and evening was a flurry of activity; Johnathon had to ride back into town for help. By the time the men, now a dozen strong, were ready to start the descent down the face of the cliff, they were forced to climb by the light of torches.

I went back and forth several times to see how things were progressing. There was a shocking contrast between all that motion and purpose outside and the strangely subdued waiting within.

Mrs. Duffy was at a loss as to how to cope with the situation. 'What do I do about dinner?' she cried. The day help, including Cook, had already left as evening approached, and the housekeeper had been trying to keep the evening meal warm.

'Let it be,' I said, hardly noticing that I was assuming authority where I had none. 'They won't want to stop now until they've found . . . until they've finished. I do think, though, that some hot soup—lots of it, enough for everyone—and some tea—would be appropriate. Can you manage that by yourself?'

'Oh, yes, certainly,' she said, glad to be relieved of decision-making responsibility. 'I'll get something cooking right away.'

By the time I had fed and put Elizabeth firmly to bed, over her objections, Mrs. Duffy had a huge pot of soup simmering on the stove and plenty of hot tea ready. Between the two of us, we got it outside and set up a makeshift kitchen. We were able to serve soup and tea to the men.

Johnathon did not eat; he was the first to descend the treacherous cliff and the last to come up. Long before he made his way back to the top, we had learned the grizzly truth from the others.

Eleanor was down there—dead. Somehow, she and her chair had gone over the cliff to the rocks far below.

CHAPTER TEN

The men and all the activity were gone. In contrast, the house, lying so still about me, seemed to be holding its breath. It was nearly midnight, some four hours since the confirmation of Eleanor's death.

I came down the stairs quietly, holding one of the kerosene lamps aloft to light my way. A flickering light from the library told me that Johnathon was there, and without hesitation, I went directly to that room.

He was standing at the window, looking out upon a black night. He must have seen my reflection in the darkened window, for as I entered the room he turned to face me.

'I wanted to tell you how sorry I am,' I said, pausing just within the room.

'Thank you,' he said gruffly. 'For all that you've done, too.'

'I've done very little, I'm afraid, but cause trouble,' I said frankly. 'But if there is anything that I've done for which gratitude is due, perhaps you will repay me by doing something for me.'

'And what is that?'

'Go to bed,' I said, a note of pleading creeping into my voice. 'It's quite late, and you must be exhausted. You've eaten nothing all day. Will you let me fix you something?'

For the first time, he smiled, albeit wanly. 'I have no doubt you are a cook as well,' he said softly.

'I can find my way about a kitchen,' I admitted with a smile of my own. 'Will you eat something?'

'I think not,' he said, the smile fading. 'But thank you just the same. As for going to bed, be assured, I will do so in good time. Now perhaps you should follow your own advice.'

'Very well,' I said, turning to go. But he stopped me by speaking my name.

'Mary,' he said in a strange way, as if he were testing the sound of it on his tongue.

'Yes?' I said.

'Forgive me, I am presumptuous to address you like that—Miss Kirkpatrick . . .'

'Mary will do as well,' I said.

Again, that faint smile. 'Very well then, Mary it is.' But he grew serious at once, lines creasing his rugged brow. 'Tell me, Mary, how could it have happened? How could she have taken that fall?'

'Why . . . I don't know. I suppose her chair got away from her . . .' I paused, unable to convince myself of that suggestion.

'You've seen her with that chair,' he said. 'It never got away from her. And that slope just wasn't that steep. Oh, yes, with the brake off, the chair could coast downhill and go over the edge. But she was in it; she could have stopped it.'

'Perhaps she was asleep,' I ventured.

'Not with the brake off,' he said. 'Anyway, she wasn't the sort to sleep in her chair in the out of doors. No, it wasn't that.'

He saw the thought that fluttered across my mind and said, quickly, 'And God knows, she was not the suicide type. You're a smart enough girl to see that for yourself.'

'You're right,' I agreed thoughtfully. 'Eleanor was the last person to take her own life.'

'Then,' he said with a weary sigh, as if he had been over all this a hundred times before, 'how did she and her chair end up at the bottom of that cliff? As if she had run it right off.'

'Perhaps she didn't, perhaps . . .?' But I caught myself as I realized what I had been going to say. 'Oh.'

His grave eyes bore into mine. 'Unless somebody else pushed her,' he said for me.

'But that's insane,' I cried. 'Who could have done that? And why would anyone do such a thing?'

'I asked myself the same thing,' he said. 'But the chair certainly did go over, and not just by running away from her either.'

'Then there is some other explanation,' I insisted. 'Perhaps she was only out for some air, was actually going somewhere, and she fainted. She hadn't eaten, after all, and it's possible she was suddenly overcome by a dizzy spell. She may have even, as she fainted, involuntarily propelled her chair forward. Wouldn't that be possible?'

He sighed again and said, 'Maybe. I don't know.' He looked away from me, around the room, as if he would find the answer written upon the walls.

At length, his gaze came back to me. 'But that is my mystery,' he said. 'And now, coleen, if you will take yourself to bed.'

I hesitated for a moment, until he added, 'I would prefer it.' With that, I could not argue, and I left him there to make my lonely way back upstairs.

I had not quite reached to the stairs when I was stopped by the sound of sobbing. It was a distant, muffled sound; Elizabeth, I thought, crying over Eleanor. Although her aunt had not been a demonstrative person, they no doubt had felt a normal affection for each other.

I retraced my steps. The old nursery was downstairs, opposite the dining room; it was Johnathon who had decreed this room for Elizabeth. At first, I had thought it a peculiar choice, but upon consideration, I thought I understood his motives. Given a choice, Elizabeth would no doubt have chosen her mother's former room, and I think Johnathon meant to avoid this by putting her as far away from that room as was possible.

The sobbing stopped as I came along the hall, but I tapped at her door nonetheless and went in. I found Elizabeth not in bed, as I had expected, but standing at an open door. This room had at one time apparently been a butler's room and had its own entrance; the door, I had been assured by Mrs. Duffy, had been locked for years because no one knew where the key was. But now it was open, and Elizabeth, in nothing but her nightgown, was standing in the chill night air.

'Good heavens,' I exclaimed, hurrying to her. 'Come out of that draft before you catch your death of cold.'

'It's not cold tonight,' she said, but she let me pilot her back to her bed and tuck her in.

'It's cold enough for young girls to get sick,' I said. 'Parading around in nothing but that! What on earth were you looking at, anyway?'

'At the cliff,' she said simply.

I felt an odd chill. I went to the door and looked out. It did indeed open upon the back, with the hill sloping down to that sheer cliff, and there between us and the edge was that twisted tree.

I shut the door rather harder than I intended. 'Where did you find the key?' I asked. 'Mrs. Duffy seemed to think there wasn't one.'

'It was unlocked,' she said. I found her regarding me with what, under any other circumstances, I would have taken to be restrained amusement. Although she was not smiling, there was a certain glint in her eyes.

'Elizabeth,' I began, but she cut me off with a long yawn.

'I think I'll go to sleep now,' she said and turned on her side, her back to me.

I hesitated for a moment; then, with a sigh, I went to her and leaned down to kiss her cheek. She murmured a sleepy 'Good night,' and I went out.

It was not until I was again in the hall that I remembered the sobbing that had originally brought me to her room.

I stopped short, staring at her closed door. There had been no evidence of crying when I went in. Had she stopped as quickly as that? Or had I been mistaken in what I thought I heard? The wind . . . or . . . ?

It was suddenly cold in the hall; an

107

unexpected draft whipped my skirt about my ankles and sent me hurrying upstairs.

On the landing, I looked up and saw the portrait of Angela. I paused, staring up at that canvas face, so lovely, so real that it too seemed to be smiling at me in barely concealed amusement.

I thought of Eleanor, so strong-willed, so determined, so opposed to having Elizabeth here. She had chastised me, cut herself off from Elizabeth, and antagonized her brother. And now she was dead.

Surely, it had been an accident. What else could it have been?

The painted eyes stared back at me, but whatever answer they had for my questions they kept to themselves.

CHAPTER ELEVEN

Nearly the whole town turned out for Eleanor's funeral. As she was lowered into the ground, they stood back at a respectful distance, a semicircle in black, watching silently. Johnathon and Elizabeth stood alone in front, and Mrs. Duffy and I stood behind them. There were no other mourners, although the commander made a respectful appearance, and Isabelle Simpson spoke briefly to Johnathon.

It seemed to me that the attitude of the townspeople was more curious and watchful than sympathetic. I had no doubt that this new tragedy had spawned another generation of rumors about Green Willows and its inhabitants. It also occurred to me that I was now one of those inhabitants. I caught several of them staring at me in an unnerving way, but they avoided my glances. Even old Miss Meriweather, who had heretofore been the friendliest of the local women, gave me no more than a barely perceptible nod.

We had not been back at Green Willows for more than an hour when Commander Whittsett arrived. I was on the stairs when Mrs. Duffy showed him in, and I was dismayed to hear his gruff voice. I knew why he had come. Since Eleanor's tragic death, I suppose I had been half expecting his visit. He had given at best a begrudging consent to allowing Elizabeth to return home; certainly, be would feel that she could not stay now.

'Commander, how nice to see you,' I said, hurrying into the parlor, where Mrs. Duffy had shown him. I gave him my best smile, hoping to thaw some of his cold reserve. I was quite unsuccessful.

'This is not a social call,' he said sharply. 'Where is Johnathon?'

'Right here,' Johnathon said. He had come in right behind me. 'What can we do for you, Commander?'

'There is no need for us to mince words with each other,' he said. 'I've come to take my granddaughter back to town.'

'Then,' Johnathon said, 'unless I can persuade you to have a glass of whisky with me, you've wasted a trip.'

There was a pregnant silence before the old man said, 'Do you mean to say you will try to prevent my taking her with me?'

'Not try,' Johnathon said calmly. 'I forbid it. She is my daughter, and I have decided that her place is here. I am sorry if that displeases you.'

That it did more than merely displease the commander was quite evident, but I breathed a mental sigh of relief to learn Johnathon's position. Thinking to avert a major battle, I stepped between the two of them.

'Forgive me for intruding,' I said, speaking quickly before I could be silenced, which I fancied the commander was about to do. 'But I feel that I have a stake in this too, as Elizabeth has been entrusted to my care. I believe that Johnathon is right. This has been a tragic occurrence, of course, but it is not fair to punish the child because of a coincidence.'

'And are you convinced that it was only coincidence,' the commander asked me.

'But of course. What else could it be?' I said. 'An accident occurred, nothing more. And accidents do occur, and people do die. However unpleasant, these are facts of life,

110

and facts that Elizabeth will sooner or later have to face. Whisking her away from here will not change that or make it any easier for her to cope with life's unpleasant realities.'

'Elizabeth is a sensitive and highly imaginative child,' the commander said angrily.

'As are most young girls,' I said.

For a long moment, he was silent, but I did not delude myself that I had convinced him. He stared at me angrily while he sought for what he wanted to say.

'Do you know what they're saying in the village?' he demanded.

'I could make a good guess,' Johnathon said. His own voice had taken on a sharp edge, and I knew that he too was growing angry.

'What can it matter what they're saying,' I asked.

'They are saying that Eleanor's death was no accident,' the commander said, all but shouting. 'They are saying . . .'

'I don't want to hear any more,' Johnathon said. His own voice was so low that one had almost to strain to hear it, and yet the intensity of his emotion was such that even the commander, who was surely not accustomed to being cut off in midsentence, left the rest of his remarks unsaid.

'Very well,' he said after another silence. 'I will leave. But we have not finished with this conversation.'

He wheeled about and strode imperiously from the room. I watched him go with a mixture of relief and sorrow. I was glad to have the scene ended and glad that Elizabeth was being allowed to stay. But I feared that the antagonism he felt for Johnathon and for myself had only been reinforced. I had hoped to be able to win his acceptance if not his friendship, but even that seemed incredibly remote just now.

'Perhaps,' I said, finding Johnathon's eyes on me, 'I should have remained silent.'

'I would rather have you speak your mind,' he said. 'Especially when it agrees with my own.'

'I cannot promise that will always be the case.'

'Then if I must quarrel, I would rather it be with you than with the commander.'

Even I had to laugh at that, and some of the tension was dissipated. But I did not forget the commander's visit or his warning.

I had not accurately gauged the extent of the feeling in the village until I again called upon Isabelle Simpson. She seemed somewhat distant when first I arrived, and as she was usually so open, I could not help but notice this at once. For the first time since we had met, there was a definite constraint between us, so after only a few minutes I rose to go.

'Perhaps it would be better if I went along to Green Willows,' I said.

112

'Do come back,' she said, rising also.

'Do you really want me to?' I asked frankly.

My frankness caught her off guard and broke down her reserve. She had the grace to look greatly embarrassed and put out a hand to touch my arm. Because she was not usually a demonstrative person, I knew that she was moved.

'I am sorry,' she said. 'How awful of me. You must think I am only another silly gossiping woman.'

'I think you are a fairly sensible woman who has probably had to listen to a great deal of gossip in the last few days,' I said, smiling.

'My dear, you've no idea,' she said, relaxing into her old self. 'Oh, come on, let's do have some tea, please. To blazes with all those women.'

We had our tea and chatted about inconsequential things. By mutual if tacit consent, we avoided talking about Green Willows or about Eleanor's death, until I was preparing some time later to leave.

'You know what they're saying,' she said when we were at the door. I shook my head. 'They're saying Eleanor was murdered.'

'How can they say that?' I asked, my voice rising in pitch. 'Who can they possibly think murdered her? Me? Elizabeth? Johnathon? And why?'

She studied me intently for a moment. 'You know people think the house is haunted.'

113

I would like to have laughed and said how ridiculous that was, but no words would come. My confusion must have shown on my face because Isabelle looked surprised.

'Mary, surely you aren't beginning to think . . . Look, nothing has happened out there to make you believe . . . that Green Willows is haunted? Because you and I know that's nonsense. We've been all through that.'

'Of course, it's nonsense,' I assured her, managing a little laugh. 'It's only, you've got to admit that it's a bit unnerving having people think the house you're in is haunted—not only haunted, but that someone there was murdered by, well, by something!'

'It's a lot of silly prattle,' she said in her no-nonsense voice. 'Just so it's not starting to get to you. It would be uncomfortable living up there if you started believing that sort of thing.'

'Yes, it would,' I agreed.

CHAPTER TWELVE

I woke to the scent of gardenias. It was as if my room had been turned into a garden of flowers, their perfume intoxicating me. I lay between sleep and waking, breathing deeply, sighing dreamily.

But there were no gardenias here, no

flowers and no perfume. When this thought penetrated my drowsiness, my eyes flew open, and I sat up in the dark room.

I think that I half expected what happened next. The sobbing began, low and plaintive, but close at hand; not in the distant nursery this time, but here, in my room. I felt the skin of my arms actually tingle.

I groped for the matches, struck one, and lit the kerosene lamp by my bed. Its yellow light revealed the room just as it had been earlier when I retired—the window I had left cracked slightly, the curtains fluttering in a faint breeze. The fire had died out, but the night was warm.

There was no one in the room with me. I had known there would not be, even before I lit the lamp. I turned my head slowly to and fro, looking into every corner, and still the sobbing went on, muffled and low, and the shadows flickered and danced. The skin crawled on the back of my neck.

It stopped, and I realized too that the scent of gardenias was gone, but I could not say how long it had been absent.

And yet, and here is the peculiar thing, while it was eerie and unnerving, I was not truly afraid. There was something so unhappy, so hopeless in that crying that it instilled pity rather than fear. You wanted to reach out, to warm, to comfort, to console. If this was a ghost, and I could hardly doubt it any longer, it was no threatening wraith, but the troubled spirit of someone who had known an anguish so great that even death had not assuaged it.

But why, then, had it come to me? What succor could I, who could hardly help those real beings about me, offer to this griever from beyond? Was there any purpose to its visit, or was it a meaningless clinging to the scene of past sorrow?

I slipped from the bed and went to close the window. I thought of Elizabeth in her distant bedroom. Before, the sobbing had come from there. Had it gone there now? And would she be frightened as I had not been? I made up my mind that I must go to her. Taking the lamp with me, I left my room and made my way to the staircase as quietly as I could.

I had hardly started down, though, when something happened. It was like stepping through a door into the icy cold of winter, for here the air was as frigid as a snowstorm. It was a palpable cold that seemed to weight one's steps and hold one back. A moment before, it had been a warm night, and now I was shivering so violently that I could hardly descend the stairs.

Nor did I especially want to. It no longer seemed important that I check on Elizabeth. What did it matter? What did anything matter? Life was a sham at best, was it not, and mine certainly had served no purpose. I was alone, unloved, unwanted, in a dreary house, nothing more than an object of curiosity to people for whom I did not care. For what was I living? Why was I struggling? To fight with the commander? To try to cram knowledge into Elizabeth's childish mind? To hope that Johnathon Tremayne might take some notice of me?

Where would it all lead but to the grave, perhaps to a death as lonely and as tragic as Eleanor Tremayne's had been. And then they would talk of me; they would say that I had joined the spirits haunting Green Willows.

Why go on then? Why not end it now and be done with it? Surely, that was the only sensible thing to do.

I had reached the landing when this thought occurred to me, and while at another time I might have laughed at it, just then it seemed to me eminently practical. I stopped in my descent and leaned over the railing, looking down at the hard wood floor far below. A long drop, undoubtedly long enough to break one's neck.

That was when I first saw her. At that, I really saw nothing but a greenish gray glow, like a mist, that seemed to rise up from the floor. It moved in a jellylike way, waving faintly to and fro, seeming to grow both in size and intensity. I thought—but this may have been a trick of my imagination—I thought I recognized a human form or at least what was shaping itself into some vague imitation of human form, but it was too indefinite to be certain.

And now I felt all of the fear, all of the spine-tingling icy horror that I had missed before. Perhaps it was my despondent state of mind that made me susceptible when I had not been earlier. But now I could feel my blood curdle in my veins, and had I been able to find my voice, I have no doubt that I would have thrown back my head and given vent to the most monstrous shrieks of terror. I know that my legs turned to water, and I found myself crouching on my knees, clinging desperately to the wooden rungs of the stair rail. I could neither run nor scream nor summon the courage to combat my terror. I could only cling helplessly and watch wide eyed as that awful apparition, made the more terrifying by its shapelessness, swelled and grew and waved.

It began to move, and I think that if it had moved toward me I would have lost all remnants of sanity, but it moved in the opposite direction, away from me along the hall. Such was my state that as I watched it go I felt a surge of relief.

At length, though, I realized where it was going—toward Elizabeth's room. And if I had feared that that gentle sobbing might frighten her, I could not bear to think what this experience might do to her.

That thought at least gave me the courage that had failed me before. I got to my feet, still clinging to the rail and breathing as though I had run all the way from the village.

I had scarcely started down the stairs when I heard a noise behind me. So tightly strung were my nerves that I gave a little scream and whirled about, almost flinging myself over the banister.

It was Johnathon, pausing at the head of the stairs before rushing down to me. For one insane moment, I thought that he meant to fling his arms about me, and I stepped toward him, meaning to throw myself into them. But he checked the impulse, if he had ever really felt it, and I caught myself a hair's breadth away from making a fool of myself.

'What are you doing here?' he demanded. 'What are you doing out of your room?'

Had he shown concern, I suspect that I would have done the only sensible thing and burst into tears, but the anger in his voice, for which I was totally unprepared, was like a dash of cold water. My back went stiff, and I said in a quite businesslike tone, 'I thought I heard something. I was going to check on Elizabeth.'

He regarded me intently for a moment. I half expected him to rebuke me and send me back to my room, and I suppose some coward-spirit in me would have been glad to go. I knew one thing, though, that if I had to go down those stairs, across the spot where I had seen that apparition, and to Elizabeth's room, I would much prefer to go in his company, although exactly how I could arrange that I had no idea.

After a long moment, though, he seemed to shrug off his anger, and the look in his eyes softened.

'You heard it too?' he asked softly.

There was no need for pretense; I knew exactly what he meant, and he knew that I knew. I nodded.

'You've heard it before?'

'Yes,' I said. I struggled with my conscience as to whether I should tell him that I had seen something, but in the long run, what could I tell him? I had not in fact seen *anything*. Now, my fear partly vanished, I could no longer be sure what I had seen—a bit of fog, perhaps, drifted in from outside, transformed by imagination and sleepfulness into something it was not.

'Come with me,' he said. He took my arm, and I went willingly down the stairs with him. I could not suppress a shudder that went through me as we reached the bottom, but look though I might, there was nothing there now. The horrible cold had vanished too, and again the night was warm.

We went straight to Elizabeth's room; perhaps my thoughts had somehow communicated themselves to him. I did not know what to expect. Certainly that Elizabeth would be awake, that she too must have heard what we heard. I could not help but think she would be frightened.

To my surprise, she was asleep. The door to the outside was open, and her room was dark but for the glow of moonlight through the open door; light enough to reveal Elizabeth curled snugly in her bed.

Johnathon went across to the door and closed it, bolting it securely. Then, stealthily, we left. There was nothing there, nothing to be seen or even sensed—no eerie chills, no mists, no sobbing. Whatever had disturbed us had apparently ignored the girl altogether. It was comforting in a sense, and yet it made me oddly uneasy. Had it not been for Johnathon, I would have been tempted to believe I had imagined everything.

'It was real, wasn't it?' I asked him when we had returned to the main hall.

'Yes,' he said. 'Come in here.'

He brought me into his library. There had been a fire on the grate earlier, and now it was burned down to smoldering ashes. He put a log on it and waited until it had begun to blaze. Despite the evening's warmth, I felt chilled, and I was grateful for the fire.

'Are you very tired?' he asked.

'I couldn't sleep just now,' I said.

'Sit here then, in front of the fire. Would you like some brandy?'

'Just a little, please.'

He brought it; far from intoxicating me it had a sobering sting that was not unwelcome.

Johnathon came to stand by the fire, one arm upon the rough mantel.

'So, now you know the secret of Green Willows,' he said at last.

'Has it always been like this?'

'Since her death,' he said, without explaining whom he meant. 'It comes and goes. At first, I thought I was going mad.'

'I know,' I said. 'At first, I was convinced I was letting my imagination run away with me. That was why you sent Elizabeth away, I suppose.'

'Yes. I would not have let her return, but everything had been so . . .' he paused. 'So quiet. I thought perhaps it was ended, that it would be safe to bring her back. But I was clearly mistaken. She'll have to return to her grandfather's cottage.'

I hesitated to speak my mind; it was my presumption, after all, that had caused Elizabeth's return, and I knew that he was being tactful in not mentioning it.

At length, I took a deep breath and plunged in. 'Must she return?' I asked.

He turned toward me and gave me a genuinely surprised look. 'What can you mean? You've heard, you know now, you must agree that it would be best.'

'I'm not sure—oh, I grant you, there is something here. Say the house is haunted, if you will. But what exactly has been done, what has really happened? We've heard someone

122

crying, that's about all. No one has been harmed.'

'Weren't you frightened?'

'Terrified for a few minutes. But Elizabeth wasn't even awakened. And why should she be, if you stop to think of it. This . . . this spirit, ghost, whatever—it must be her mother, must it not? Forgive me, I know that I speak of your wife, if I am too bold . . . ?'

'Go on,' he said, listening with interest.

'Everyone speaks of her as an angel, and she is Elizabeth's mother. Surely, she would not wish any harm to her child.'

'Yet harm need not always be intentional,' he said.

'Yes, but if Elizabeth does not even hear her, is not even aware of the visitation, as apparently she was not tonight? And consider, if you send her away, how will you explain it so that you will not do even more harm. You must offer some explanation, and to tell her the truth, would only leave her more obsessed with Green Willows and the spirit of her dead mother. Yet anything less than the truth would certainly drive her from you forever.'

He was thoughtful for a long time. I sat in silence, waiting for some reply from him.

He said, more to the fire than to me, 'Certainly, it would be difficult to explain to the commander.'

'He would send her away; we both know that,' I said.

123

He turned to face me directly again. 'Have you no reservations?' he asked.

'Indeed,' I confessed. 'As I had reservations when I came here. But I set them aside until I could see what the true situation was. And I suggest we do the same now.'

He sighed and finished off his brandy. 'You are a persuasive woman. I will do as you suggest—for now. But I tell you now, if danger threatens I will not hesitate to send both her and you away.'

He thought a second or two before adding, 'But I am being selfish because I need you here. Perhaps after tonight you would prefer to leave?'

I had to fight not to show my pleasure at his remark; I had never in my life been told that anyone needed me. Aloud, I said, 'I will stay.'

I rose to leave, but he put out a hand to delay me. Our eyes met. I was afraid to interpret the look in his and hopeful that my full feelings did not show in mine.

'I am glad,' he said in a voice unlike any he had used with me before.

I did not linger to explore that further. I murmured good night and went back to my room.

My heart felt filled to overflowing.

CHAPTER THIRTEEN

In the light of day, my memory of the night seemed so incredible that I was half tempted to dismiss it all as a bad dream. Had Johnathon not figured in it, I would probably have done so, but to cast out one part of the night was to cast out the other, and I was not going to part so lightly with the memory of being told that he needed me.

During breakfast, I asked Elizabeth how she had slept; I suppose it was some perverse sort of vanity that made it so difficult for me to accept that something that frightened me so thoroughly should have no effect on someone else.

'I slept soundly,' she said. 'I don't think I could sleep badly here.'

'No bad dreams?' I persisted, buttering some bread.

'Not bad dreams, only the nicest ones,' she said. 'Sometimes—I don't know how to explain this, really, but it's like I'm not dreaming at all.'

'What do you mean?' I asked, rather too sharply.

'Just that. I dream, and then I feel as if I were awake, but not entirely.'

'And what do you dream?'

'About my mother. Last night I dreamed

that she came into my room. I've dreamed that every night since I've been back.'

I tried to make myself sound calm and unconcerned. 'And does her visit frighten you?'

She looked so astonished at the suggestion that it was all I could do to keep from fully explaining the reason for my questions.

'Frighten me? But how could she?' she asked. 'It's when she comes that I stop being frightened.'

'Then you have been frightened?' I asked, alarmed by this.

She laughed and shook her head. 'Not really, not now. That's more like part of the dream. And part of what I remember from before.'

'When you were a baby, you mean? But surely, you were too young to remember any of that.'

'I don't. I mean, I don't remember anything specific. But there are impressions, things that I think I almost remember. I can remember being frightened, for one thing. And I remember my mother coming to me, comforting me.'

'And that's all?'

She shrugged and shook her head. 'It's only impressions really. But that's what my dreams have been like. I'm asleep, but I feel as if I were awake. And I'm frightened. I don't know by what. And then it's like she's there. I can't see her or anything, but it's something you just

126

know. And I feel comforted.'

'And you hear nothing?' I asked guardedly.

'No. But I smell her perfume—the gardenia scent. That I do remember from childhood.' She thought for a minute before she added, 'I may have heard her, once—I heard someone humming that little song she used to hum to comfort me.'

'In your dream, you mean?'

She gave me a peculiar look. 'Yes, of course,' she said. 'Only, it's so real.'

This conversation only served to confirm what I already believed about the haunting of Green Willows. Surely, this was Elizabeth's mother, and far from representing a threat to the girl, her presence was a comfort. Why I should have been so frightened was another question, but I was certain that the presence of Angela Tremayne was no danger.

I could not have been more foolish.

Heretofore, I had been of two minds on the matter of the hauntings and had failed to see the contradiction. While I recognized the presence of something in the house and theorized about who it was and why it was there, I continued to think of this as something that affected only myself and Johnathon and, most of all, of course, Elizabeth. I scoffed at the outsiders who feared Green Willows and regarded the place as haunted.

It was Mrs. Duffy who brought me face to face with a fact so obvious that I ought to have seen it at once—that what I could see and experience, others could likewise see and experience.

I had observed that since Eleanor's death the housekeeper had been growing strangely distant. Whereas before she had been friendly and loquacious, she had become quiet and uncommunicative. Sometimes she answered sharply when spoken to, and she no longer stopped at the slightest encouragement to exchange gossip or complaints.

I had begun to wonder about this and had set myself to try to draw her out but had thus far met with little success. On this particular morning, I especially sought her out with the excuse of thanking her for the extra comforter she had found for my bed.

'I don't know how you manage to get everything done,' I said, 'taking care of this entire house without any full-time help.'

'It isn't the work I mind,' she said, responding not at all to the compliment. 'But there are things as a body shouldn't be expected to put up with.'

'I certainly hope I've done nothing to offend,' I said quickly. 'And I'm sure that if Mr. Tremayne has it was not his intention. I'm certain he appreciates your efforts as much as I, if not more.'

'Oh, Mr. Tremayne is a good man to work for,' she said. 'Regardless of what anyone has to say about him. He's been decent to me. No,

128

it isn't him. It isn't anybody, miss, leastways not any *person*. But this house—I tell you, there's things that go beyond the call of duty. Not that I'm a scaredy cat, mind you, but enough is enough.'

These remarks were so unexpected that I was quite nonplussed, but after a moment, I recovered myself to ask, 'Why, what on earth do you mean, has something happened to frighten you?'

She gave me a sideways glance, measuring me, I thought; but all she said was, 'There now, I'm not one to go spreading stories, and I surely hope I didn't frighten you, miss. Don't you go imagining things now.'

With that, she left me. I could only ponder her remarks and conclude that I had not been alone in observing the manifestations of ghostly spirits in the house.

This gave me a new cause for concern, as I wondered what Mrs. Duffy might have seen and to whom she might have related it. I knew that she had friends in the village with whom she liked to visit, and I knew she was certainly not above a bit of gossip, notwithstanding her reluctance to tell me what had occurred. A new flurry of stories about Green Willows, especially generated by someone who lived in the house, could do no good, and if they reached the ears of Commander Whittsett, they might well do harm.

I went to our lessons that morning in a

somewhat despondent mood, which deepened as the day progressed. I found myself sharp and irritable with Elizabeth, who was at first puzzled, then hurt by my attitude.

'If you absolutely refuse to learn,' I snapped at one difficult point, 'I can hardly see any point in continuing to waste our time on grammar. Perhaps you will do better to read some history.'

I could see tears threatening, but she took her history book out wordlessly and began to study the *History of the English People*. I immediately felt guilty for my cross tone, and I was puzzled, as it was so unlike myself. I was on the verge of apologizing and suggesting that we forego our lessons for the day, but some perverse impulse stopped me.

'Let her sulk,' I thought peevishly. 'A little discipline would be a good thing for her.'

I brought out my own book and prepared to read while Elizabeth learned her English kings. But I found my attention wandering from the book. Outside, it was a bright, sunny day, and I found myself resenting being cooped up with a recalcitrant student when I would rather have been out enjoying myself. What would it benefit either of us, this worry about men who had lived and died centuries before?

I put my book aside and strode impatiently to the window. From here, I could look down upon the lake with its gazebo and the willows rustling slightly in the breeze.

'Will my father restore the gazebo, do you think?' Elizabeth asked.

I whirled about and said, 'I think you would do better to apply yourself to the assignments I have given you.'

She looked as surprised and as hurt as if I had slapped her, and in a moment, the tears that had threatened before began to fall.

I was at once ashamed of my behavior and mortified. I went to her and threw my arms about her, hugging her to me.

'Darling, I'm sorry,' I said. 'I don't know what's gotten into me. Forgive me, please.'

She was quick to accept my apology, and our little quarrel was patched up. But I did decide to let our lessons go for now and sent her out to enjoy the sunshine.

'Why don't you talk to your father about the gazebo,' I suggested. 'I'm sure he would be glad to restore it for you if he knew of your interest.'

In my own room, I thought of my strange mood; it was unlike myself, and after a time, I began to wonder if it was in some way the result of the haunting presence in the house. I remembered my eerie experience on the stairs, when I had been despondent to the point of flinging myself over the railing. Could it be that the spirits here manifested themselves in several ways, among them that chilling sense of defeat and hopelessness that had afflicted me twice already? If that was so, then perhaps I ought to reconsider my suggestion that Elizabeth be allowed to remain at Green Willows? Perhaps, after all, it would be best if she returned to her grandfather's cottage.

And I? What would I do if that happened? I felt certain that if Elizabeth returned to her grandfather he would seize the opportunity to send her away to school as he had wanted to do all along. My services would no longer be needed, and I would be dismissed. Surely, I could not stay on here in the house when the reason for my presence was ended.

I might never see Johnathon Tremayne again.

I found this thought no less disturbing than my previous bout of depression, and seizing my cape and hat, I decided that I would go for a stroll. Instinctively, I made my way to Isabelle Simpson's cottage.

I found her baking, not her usual occupation. 'I thought I might as well try my hand at some cakes,' she said, ushering me into her warm, scented kitchen. 'I won't inflict them on you; they're really quite dreadful, but we've gotten used to them.'

I laughed and insisted that I would not leave until I had tried one. 'I'm sure they're nowhere near so bad as you make out,' I said.

She made a face and said, 'Worse. But it's your stomach. I'll put on some tea.'

When the tea was brewed, though, and I

had tried her cakes, which were passably good, Isabelle grew more serious.

'Mary, what is going on up at the house?' she asked.

'What do you mean?'

'Just that. Mrs. Duffy has been spreading tales—I'm getting them all third and fourth hand, so it's hard to know just what to credit them. Apparently, she's been seeing things and hearing things, and—I swear someone actually told me this—smelling things. And you, well, if you'll pardon the expression, you really look like you've seen a ghost.'

It was enough to make me choke on a cake. When I was able to talk, however, I made up my mind to make a full confession, and I began to tell Isabelle of all the ghostly occurrences since I had arrived at Green Willows.

She listened soberly, once or twice interrupting to ask a cogent question. I half wondered if she would think I had taken leave of my senses, but I did not let that stop me from continuing to the end.

When I had finished, she was thoughtful for a moment. Finally, she said, 'Well, it certainly is a sensational story. But, Mary, ghosts?'

I sighed and said, 'I know, I know. I thought for a while I must be going mad. But I know what I've heard and what I've seen. Isabelle, I tell you, there is something haunting that house, and I believe it's Elizabeth's dead

133

mother.'

'Perhaps if I spoke to my brother . . .'

'No, please, don't. He would be duty bound, don't you see, to take some sort of action, and if Johnathon knew I had spoken to someone else, even you, he would be furious.'

'But you have to do something,' she said.

'Do we? I'm not so sure.'

'The girl . . . ?'

I shrugged. Having shared my story with someone else, it seemed far less burdensome than it had when it was mine alone. 'As far as I can see, Elizabeth is in no danger. She hasn't been threatened or frightened of all. If anything, she is comforted by the presence in the house. I believe it has been visiting her when she is asleep. I think that half awake she senses its presence and is instinctively frightened by it, but then her mother somehow comforts her, reassures her. She probably didn't do that with me because she felt no need to, I'm nothing to her, after all. At any rate, Elizabeth is reassured on some psychic level and drifts back to sleep quite contentedly.'

'I have to admit it sounds right, but still, I don't like it. I don't like any of it. If it were me, I'd have my bags packed by now.'

I smiled. I had not said anything to Isabelle of my growing attachment to Johnathon Tremayne. Even had things been considerably worse, I would have been inclined to stick it

134

out for Johnathon's sake.

It was not until I was preparing to leave, feeling better than when I had arrived, that Isabelle threw a particularly worrisome thought at me.

'We are forgetting something important,' she said, seeing me to the door. 'Eleanor's death.'

'What has that to do with anything?' I asked.

'I don't know. I hope nothing. But there was some question about how she died, and we agreed at the time that there was simply no one who would or could have pushed her. This changes things, don't you think.'

'You mean . . .' I hesitated, too astonished by the possibility she had raised to even want to voice it. 'You surely don't think that a ghost . . .'

'Pushed her? It is farfetched, I'll admit. But suppose she saw or felt what you did. Suppose she too was made despondent or frightened out of her wits, even driven . . . well, let's go ahead and say it—driven sufficiently out of her mind to fling herself over that cliff.'

I wanted to say that the suggestion was preposterous, but I was remembering my own experience on the stairs; it would have taken very little more to drive me to take my own life. Had something very similar, but worse, happened to Eleanor? It was not a possibility I liked to consider, and yet there it was.

In the end, I went home more concerned than when I had left.

CHAPTER FOURTEEN

Elizabeth did talk to her father about the gazebo; I was a little uncertain what his reaction would be to her suggestion that it be restored since it certainly must represent unpleasant memories for him, but apparently his daughter's interest outweighed other considerations. I saw the two of them strolling around the island, talking and pointing enthusiastically, and it was easy to see they were making plans, grandiose ones it would seem, for restoring the entire island.

Since Elizabeth's return, notwithstanding the strange things that had been happening, I had at least been pleased to observe that a new spirit of affection was growing up rapidly between father and daughter. Their long and, to Elizabeth, unexplained estrangement would not be overcome in a few days, but fortunately, each had always been willing to recognize his love for the other, and this would help them.

But what, I asked myself unhappily, would happen if they should have to be separated again? If Green Willows was a threat to Elizabeth—and I was far from willing to admit this now—then she would have to be removed.

Whether Johnathon would give up his home and go elsewhere with her, I did not know; in any event, it would certainly end my relationship with both of them.

If only I had a better understanding of what had gone on in the house so long ago. Perhaps in those past events was a clue that would help me; why was Elizabeth's mother clinging to Green Willows even beyond death? Was it only a strong attachment to the place, or did she, like her father, the commander, feel that Johnathon was inadequate as a father? Was she perhaps remaining so that she could, in a manner of speaking, keep an eye on her beloved daughter? Or was there something else, something out of that tragic story Isabelle had told me?

I longed to ask Johnathon the truth about the events that had transpired at Green Willows, but he was not a talkative man at best and would certainly have been justified in chastising me for putting my nose into his personal affairs.

*   *   *

It was a few days after I had told Isabelle about the haunting of Green Willows that I received a letter that removed my thoughts, for a time, from the subject; indeed, it removed me physically from Green Willows as well.

I received a letter telling me that my aunt in Brighton was quite ill and suggesting that, as her only relative, I should attempt to journey there as quickly as possible, as the doctor could not say how much time she might have.

'Take all the time you need,' Johnathon said when I showed him the letter. 'Have you enough money?'

'Quite enough, thank you,' I assured him; since my arrival I had spent little of the generous salary he was paying me and so had saved a tidy nest egg.

'When would you like to leave?' he asked.

'The letter indicates that speed is advisable. I thought perhaps tomorrow,' I said.

'I'll make the arrangements for you,' he said.

On the following day, I kissed Elizabeth, who was tearful at my leaving. Cook and Mrs. Duffy wished me well in solicitous tones, although I think Mrs. Duffy was rather sorrier for herself being left without companionship of sorts.

It felt peculiar to be saying good-bye to Johnathon in such a formal manner. He wished me a safe journey and added to my surprise, 'We shall miss you very much until you return.'

With those words singing in my heart, I left for Brighton.

By the time I had completed that lengthy journey, in bad weather moreover, nothing within me was singing. Brighton is a seaside resort and is no doubt lovely in season—I had never been so fortunate as to see it then—but it was now winter, and the cold winds blew in from the sea without mercy.

I found that my aunt, who had been rather near death, had recovered enough to be conscious and to recognize me. We had never been particularly close, but I think she was grateful I had come; no one likes to die alone.

'I expect your stay will not be a long one,' she told me in a hoarse whisper.

'The doctors say there is hope,' I said, repeating what the housekeeper had told me.

'The doctors,' she said scornfully. 'Pshaw.' She went into a violent coughing fit and was not able to converse with me further that day.

It was not until my second day there that, my aunt sleeping, I was able to go out for a breath of air, and I discovered the School of Angela's Kindness. It was an imposingly ugly building that sat by itself at the end of a little narrow street. On one side, it was joined to the neighboring building, but on the other was a narrow walkway at the end of which I could see an iron fence and a corner of what looked to be a playground. Schools are often grim-looking places, but this one was particularly so, and I wondered what sort of school it was. The name Angela at first only struck me as coincidence, until later when I talked for a while with my aunt.

She was again feeling well enough to sit up for a bit and carry on some conversation, and I found myself asking her about the school.

'It's such an odd-looking place—do you know anything about it?' I asked.

'Enough to know that it's more than odd looking,' she said. 'Strange woman runs it—came down from your part of the country years ago, it seems to me. Mrs. Woodburn or something like that.'

It was only then that I remembered what Isabelle had told me; after Angela Tremayne's death, her nurse and companion, Mrs. Woodridge, had come to Brighton where she now ran a girls' school.

'Mrs. Woodridge?' I asked.

'Yes, that's it, Woodridge. Fierce old dragon, they tell me. Way I hear it, they teach spiritual enlightenment, harmony of the spirit— you know, that kind of nonsense.'

'How interesting,' was all I said.

*   *   *

I was two weeks at Brighton. My aunt's recovery was brief, and it was followed by a relapse from which she did not again rally. She died quietly in her sleep and was buried two days after. I stayed to make the arrangements and to put things in order.

My aunt had not been a wealthy woman, although I inherited a comfortable sum and

140

the house. The rest went to her housekeeper, who had been with her for many years, and to the church.

It was not until all this business was concluded that I did what I had made up my mind to do almost from the day I had learned who was the owner of the School of Angela's Kindness; I paid a call upon Mrs. Woodridge.

CHAPTER FIFTEEN

The School of Angela's Kindness was, if anything, grimmer on the inside than on the outside. There were no paintings on the walls, no students' crayon drawings pasted up for encouragement. The halls were dark brown, lighted by a single overhead light. The floors were bare and dark. The rooms that I spied opening off the corridor were spartan. Angela's Kindness, apparently, did not run to cheery settings.

'I'll see,' was the dubious response from the birdlike creature who answered the door when I asked to see Mrs. Woodridge. 'She rarely sees outsiders. Is this about a pupil?'

'A former pupil, in a manner of speaking,' I said after a moment's hesitation. 'Tell her I am from Green Willows.'

It was evident that the message meant nothing to her, but undoubtedly, it did to

Mrs. Woodridge. The maid was back in a minute, looking quite awed and a little frightened.

'She'll see you right away,' she said. 'This way, please.'

I glanced to right and left as we marched along the corridor. There were girls in some of the rooms, and I heard snatches of lectures. Several of the girls glanced furtively around as we passed, and I heard a sharp voice reprimand one of them. I smelled chalk, disinfectant, and stale air.

Mrs. Woodridge's own office was a contrast. Here large windows in two walls let in plenty of light, and the curtains were bright and cheery looking. There was an expensive-looking carpet on the floor, and a massive desk dominated the entire room.

Mrs. Woodridge dominated the desk. She was seated behind it when I came in, just as she no doubt was when a recalcitrant pupil was brought before her. I felt as if I were such a one; the effect was much as if I were being brought before judgment, and I fancied that this was an intentional effect. She did not rise at first; indeed, for a moment, she continued to work at the papers before her. The woman who had brought me in hopped back out again, and the door closed.

At the sound, Mrs. Woodridge stood up, seemingly discovering my presence for the first time. She did not smile, but she rose and came about the desk to meet me, extending a firm hand to shake mine.

'Miss Kirkpatrick,' she said. 'Won't you have a chair, please.'

I made the mistake of sitting down; she did not. She remained standing so that she towered over me most imposingly. I was intimidated at once, as she no doubt intended.

Mrs. Woodridge would have been an intimidating creature under any circumstances. She was big—not fat, but big, as big as a man—and exuded a forthright air of authority. Her hands were strong and square, with thick, blunt fingers that her many rings did not succeed in making feminine. Her dress too sat incongruously upon her vast frame. Her face was chiseled and lined, but firm of jaw, and her eyes were ageless, fiery orbs that seemed to penetrate to your inmost thoughts. Her thick glasses made her eyes appear smaller and at the same time more intense.

'You have come, I suppose, as an emissary for Mr. Tremayne,' she said, taking immediate charge of the conversation.

'No. In fact, he does not even know I am here,' I said. I fancied that she relaxed somewhat, although relaxation was perhaps too strong a word to apply to Mrs. Woodridge. To my mind, it was doubtful that those firm shoulders ever drooped, that her rigid spine ever slackened.

I explained quickly in hurried phrases, of my

aunt's illness and of my discovery that the school was linked to a former resident of Green Willows.

When I finished, I paused uncertainly, not knowing in the face of that cold scrutiny just what I had hoped to accomplish here.

'Why have you come here, then?' she asked. 'Surely not from idle curiosity.' Her tone implied that that was such a grievous explanation that it pained her even to suggest it.

I took the bull by the horns, saying, 'Mrs. Woodridge, I have come because things at Green Willows puzzle me, and I believe perhaps you can help me to understand them better.'

'What sort of things puzzle you?' she asked.

'I would like to know what happened when you were there. You are perhaps the only person who really knows the circumstances surrounding Mrs. Tremayne's death. Will you tell me about that?'

She regarded me steadily for a full minute, and I understood how her pupils felt when brought before her for questioning.

'And why should I tell you about that?' she asked. 'It is a painful subject for me, and I fail to see what good it can do you. That was long ago.'

'But it affects the here and now,' I said stubbornly. 'Especially, it affects Elizabeth Tremayne—Angela's daughter. I am here for her sake, not for my own.'

'Ah,' she said, nodding as if in a twinkling she had grasped everything. 'The child. How is she?'

'She is fine, I think. She's a bright child and a good girl. I never knew her mother, but Elizabeth must be just as pretty as Angela was.'

'Never,' Mrs. Woodridge said with so angry a conviction that I feared that I had just defeated myself. 'No one was as pretty as Angela; no one ever will be.'

But she paused and added, 'I am sure Elizabeth is attractive, though; she took after her mother, fortunately.'

I bit my tongue to keep from responding to that; I already feared I was found wanting.

'I should have had her here,' she said in a suddenly accusing tone. 'This is what her mother wanted for her. She would have wanted me in charge of the girl's education. I suppose you are her governess?'

'Yes. I have tried to give her a good education. As I said, she's quite bright, and she learns quickly.'

'All the wrong things,' Mrs. Woodridge said rudely. She turned from me and went to the window. I could see from where I sat that a number of girls had filed out into the yard behind the school, but no one seemed to be playing or enjoying herself. I heard no girlish laughter, no squeals of delight or shouted invitations to play.

'All the wrong things,' she murmured again, gazing at the girls outside. Suddenly, she turned back to me.

'Why have you come,' she demanded. 'What is wrong at Green Willows that has sent you here?'

I swallowed and said, 'Because I have reason to believe that Angela is still at Green Willows. I think her spirit has never left it.'

She did not, as I had feared, laugh or scorn. She only nodded as if I had told her something patently obvious.

'Of course,' she said. 'She would not leave, could not leave, with her child still in his power. Even the grave was not so strong as her love, her goodness. He is an evil man. She knows that. How she knows that!'

'Perhaps she does,' I said levelly. 'But I do not unless you are willing to tell me. Why is Angela there? What does she want or what does she fear? Surely, you cannot suggest that Mr. Tremayne wishes any harm to his child.'

'You think not,' she snapped.

'I am confident that he loves Elizabeth, and she loves him,' I said.

'As he loved his wife, who also loved him?' She gave me a scornful smirk. 'Oh, yes, I know all about his love. It destroyed her, his love, his all too encompassing love.'

She strode purposefully across the room and, to my surprise, seated herself on a black leather divan, facing me. She even leaned slightly forward as a gesture of intimacy.

'Very well,' she said. 'I shall tell you. Then you'll see what I mean.'

She paused, tilting her head back and closing her eyes as if to summon up those scenes of old. 'Never,' she said, 'was there anyone so virtuous, so good, so beautiful as my Angela. I was her nurse when she was an infant. I never left her, not once in her entire life. I was abroad with her parents, and when the commander's wife died and he came back to England, I came with them. Angela was my life. Nothing could have taken her from me, nothing but . . .'

She left that sentence unfinished and again turned those gleaming eyes upon me. 'He tried. With his whispered words and his bestial caresses, he tried to lead her from the path I had prepared for her, the path of virtue, the path of goodness. I tried to tell her, I railed, I argued, but she would marry him. Very well, then, I said, marry him, but I'll not leave your side. And I didn't, ever.

'We moved to Green Willows. She was like a queen there. Everyone worshipped her.' She added, unnecessarily, 'I most of all.

'But she was not strong, you know. Her health had always been frail, and he—the demands he made upon her, his animalistic appetites—they robbed her of her strength. Even I could not maintain her health there. I told her that she must go abroad, without him, to recuperate. She knew that I was right, as usual, and we went.'

She paused again. Whenever she spoke of Angela, Mrs. Woodridge's features softened and took on a beatific glow, but now she grimaced with remembered disgust.

'There was a girl in Italy, a coarse, peasant who worked in the house we were staying in. Angela set eyes on her—anyone else would have seen her for a wanton—but to Angela no one was beyond redemption. She took the girl under her wing. Oh, I told her, there are some people who just can't he helped—they're like the poor, they'll always be with us, the Master himself said that.

'But there was no reasoning with Angela on this. She meant to help this girl, and she would let nothing discourage her. She brought her back to Green Willows with us. By then she'd had Elizabeth; we didn't discover till we were in Italy that she was expecting. I forbade her to let her husband come to her. It was his fault anyway, and I was so afraid she wouldn't survive the birth. If it hadn't been for me, she might not have either.'

She delivered this last as an announcement and stopped long enough for me to show proper appreciation. 'She grew into a very healthy girl, I'd say,' I told her.

She made a snorting sound. 'And Angela nearly died,' she said. She was silent for so long that I thought perhaps she had lost the thread of her story, and I prompted her.

'Was Angela successful in her plans for Gina?'

'That witch.' She spat the words at me. 'You want to know how successful she was? That Italian she-cat killed her. Murdered her. The one person in the world who had ever tried to help her. That's how successful she was.'

'But surely, you don't mean that literally,' I protested.

'Don't I? I've never meant anything more literally in my life.'

'But . . . but why would she do such a thing? Surely . . .'

'Because she was engaged in a liaison with Angela's husband, for one thing.'

'Oh,' I gasped. Of course, I had heard that there had been some gossip, but there is always gossip. To hear it from someone who had been there, though, was a shock. However much Mrs. Woodridge hated Johnathon and idolized Angela, her remark still carried the power of an actual witness.

'From the day we came home,' she went on, pleased to see that she had shocked me, 'she began making eyes at him, and he at her. Oh, I saw it from the first. I caught them winking at each other, exchanging little glances. I'm no fool. I tried to tell Angela, but she wouldn't hear of it. She was so good, so trusting. She couldn't believe everyone else wasn't just like her. But I watched and waited, and one day, when they were together, I brought Angela to see.'

I felt my last hope sink. Johnathon, I cried silently within myself, how could you?

'They were actually . . . together?' I asked aloud.

'She was in his arms,' she said, smacking her lips. 'He was kissing her.'

I gave an involuntary little sigh and leaned back again in my seat. When I spoke, it was in a strangely businesslike voice. 'And Angela . . . what did she say then?'

'She was rightfully angry. She told that trollop that she would have to leave. She was very forgiving, of course, but you can understand her position. It would have been unfair, she said, to keep temptation before her weak husband. Even then, you see, she tried to excuse him, to take the blame on herself.'

'And Gina went?'

'Not before she had shown her truly heinous nature by trying to steal the baby.'

I gasped. 'Elizabeth?'

'The very one. I've never told anyone of that; there was no reason to. By the time I could have, Angela was dead, murdered and nothing mattered then. She tried to steal the baby that very night, but Angela caught her. This time she was truly angry, like an avenging angel. She unleashed her wrath upon that foreign hussy. "Find Mr. Tremayne," she told

150

me, and I left her. It was the only time I had ever left her. Would that I hadn't.'

She lowered her head, and I fancied that she was blaming herself in some way for what happened.

'I never spoke to her again,' she said. 'Gina fled the house. Angela followed her. I don't know exactly why. Perhaps she was going to forgive her even then, bring her back. They reached the lake. I looked out of a window and saw the two of them. Gina struck her—struck Angela! Angela tried to defend herself, but she had never been strong. She slipped and fell into the water. I saw her struggle; she couldn't swim. "Help her," I shouted from the window. "Help her, she can't swim."'

'And she didn't?' I asked softly.

Her eyes burned fiercely into mine. 'She laughed,' she said. 'And then she knelt down and held Angela under the water.'

I felt a wave of sickness sweep over me. I closed my eyes, and at once, I saw the lake, the bridge over it, the gazebo. I could see the two women, the one struggling desperately in the water, the other leaning down cruelly, laughing . . .

'And Johnathon,' I said, unaware that I had used his first name. 'Where was he?'

'When I finally found him, he was in his study,' she said with a shrug. 'I bet you he heard all the ruckus, watched the scene exactly as I did. But did he do anything to save his wife? He was a murderer the same as her, if you ask me.'

CHAPTER SIXTEEN

I traveled dispiritedly back to Green Willows.

I had begun to think I understood the hauntings there. For some time, I had been toying with the idea that there was not one but two ghosts at Green Willows—one, that of Angela, seeking her baby daughter, perhaps tied to the place where she died such a cruel death; and the other, Gina, evil, vengeful. This theory would explain the different reactions to the spirits that I had felt, and Mrs. Woodridge's story had strengthened this idea in my mind.

Unfortunately, though, I felt that the problem could no longer be mine. After what I had learned of Johnathon, I could not continue to remain in his house.

I was perfectly willing, of course, to admit that Mrs. Woodridge was prejudiced and quite capable of stretching the truth to flatter Angela or condemn Johnathon. But if I knew the truth at all when I heard it, she had told the truth about seeing Gina and Johnathon kissing. I had no desire to remain in the home of a man who, even while his wife was alive and in the house, engaged in amorous play with his servants.

But how, I wondered, was I to tell him this, and what was I to say to Elizabeth?

I did not see him upon my return, although I knew that he was in his study and was sure that he would expect me to make some sort of acknowledgment of my return. I went directly to my room and put away the few things with which I had traveled.

Mrs. Duffy came up a short time later. 'I was sorry to hear about your dear aunt,' she said. 'But I'm glad you're back, miss.'

I hesitated when she asked if I would be having dinner with the master or if I preferred something sent up to my room.

'It may be you're tired from all that traveling,' she suggested, seeing my uncertainty. 'A nice bit of hot soup and early to bed wouldn't hurt anything.'

'Thank you, but no. I will be down,' I said finally. I would have to face Johnathon sooner or later, and the dinner table was as good a place as any.

I could see that he was puzzled by my aloofness, but as Elizabeth was dining with us, he tactfully avoided asking directly about it. She was delighted to see me and filled with eager questions, which I tried to answer as cheerfully as possible. This was not helped by my awareness of Johnathon's constant scrutiny of me.

When, after dinner, Elizabeth suggested I

might want to see how she had done with the work I had assigned her in my absence,' her father said, 'I think that I'll wait for tomorrow. Mary has had a long journey, and I am sure she is tired.'

Elizabeth gave a disappointed sigh, but at a nod from her father, she excused herself from the table and retired to her own room.

'I was sorry to hear about your aunt,' Johnathon said when we were alone.

'Thank you,' I said, toying with my glass, and, 'No, thank you,' when he offered me more wine.

'No doubt your journey was arduous in every way,' he said. 'Why don't you take a few days to rest before starting on Elizabeth's lessons again?'

'That won't be necessary,' I said, looking along the table to meet his gaze directly for the first time. 'As a matter of fact, I am planning another trip. I thought a modest tour of the continent. I've never traveled, you know, and my aunt left me a little sum.'

He stared back at me with a quite dumbfounded expression, no doubt expecting some further explanation. When it was not forthcoming, he said, 'And when had you planned to take this trip?'

'As soon as possible,' I said, wavering before that steady gaze. I looked down at my hands; they were trembling.

After another lengthy silence, he said, 'In

other words, you are planning to leave us. That is the substance of your message, is it not?'

I nodded mutely. I did not trust my voice to speak to him.

He filled his glass again with an angry gesture, spilling the wine. It made a crimson lake upon the white dinner cloth. He got up and went to stand at the fireplace, staring hard into the leaping flames.

'Is it always so with a woman?' he asked softly, as if speaking to the fire and not to me. 'She comes into your life, all unexpected loveliness and gentleness. She smiles and coaxes and teases and works her way into your heart, where you never wanted her at all, until you can think of nothing else but her, until you dream of her each night and see her face each morning when you awaken, until every bird's song is her voice, and every flower seems to bloom only for her.'

He turned then from the fire and looked at me. 'You were the only flower in my entire, bleak life,' he said.

Suddenly, with a violent gesture, he flung his glass into the fire. The glass shattered; the fire hissed and danced, blue and green and yellow.

'Take your trip,' he said angrily. 'Leave us, go where you will, when you will, and to hell with you.'

He strode from the room, leaving me

turning an empty glass around and around in my hand. I was so astonished that for a moment I could only sit and stare bewildered after him.

Johnathon loves me. At last, the words formed themselves in my heart, timidly, hesitantly at first, and then like the bold song of a lark rising up with the dawn to herald a new day breaking. Johnathon loves me.

I said it aloud, scarcely believing, 'He loves me,' and suddenly, I leaped to my feet.

Mrs. Duffy came in just then to clear away. She gave me a startled look as I seized her and whirled her about once.

'He loves me,' I said, laughing, and she said with amazing aplomb, 'Indeed, miss.'

I ran from the room calling his name, but he was not in his study or in the parlor or in the library. 'Johnathon,' I called, running from room to room; then I realized where he would be.

The moon was waxing. It made a lopsided disc in the sky, but its light clearly showed me the lawn sloping down to the lake, the water shimmering silver, the willows like ancient sentinels, trailing their leaves upon the water.

He was in the gazebo. His back was to me, but he heard me run across the bridge and turned toward me. I stopped at the marble steps, staring up at him. The moonlight was not right for him; it made a marble mask of his face, too perfect, and this was not a perfect man, only the man that I loved.

'I suppose now you've come to taunt me,' he said in a voice drained of all emotion.

'No,' I said. I came to where he was, put a hand upon his shoulder, and leaned my cheek against his strong chest. 'No, not to taunt you.'

CHAPTER SEVENTEEN

Later, nestled comfortably in Johnathon's arms before the fire, I told him of my visit to Mrs. Woodridge and of the story she had told me. He heard me out without interruption, as I had requested; it embarrassed me to have to tell it, and I knew that once stopped I would not again be able to pick up the thread.

When I was finished, he was thoughtful for several minutes. At last, he said, 'I am ashamed to have to tell you that some of it is true.'

'The part about Gina and you . . . ?' I began.

'That is true,' he said, and when I tried to pull away from him, 'No, wait, it's true as far as it goes, that's all. You've listened to everyone else's version of things; at least listen to mine before you judge me.'

'You're right. I haven't been fair,' I said. 'But I am willing to listen now.'

He got up to stir the fire. 'I've never talked of any of this to anyone else,' he said. 'Not even the local constable. But I owe it to you.'

He put aside the poker with a vehement gesture. 'You've heard so much about Angela, about what an angel she was. Well, it's true in a sense, she was an angel. She was also an iceberg, not a woman. Her virtue, as directed by Mrs. Woodridge, permitted her to share my bed just once, for the sake of an heir, and never again after that. I wasn't allowed near her. I wasn't even permitted to kiss her. That was encouraging licentiousness.'

I could well see that this would be difficult for a man of Johnathon's temperament. 'I've always felt it would be difficult for me to live with anyone so angelic,' I said.

'And you, at least, are virtuous, where I've never pretended to be,' he said with a rueful smile. 'You can't dream what it was like. Hers was a stifling, stern puritanism. Laughter was suspect, love was strictly between herself and God, leisure was sin. To her way of thinking, half an hour spent lying in the grass looking up at the clouds guaranteed an eternity in hell.'

'It must have been terribly uncomfortable for you,' I said.

'It was my bed. I'd made it, and I was willing to lie in it. But I knew from the first it was a mistake, and I could do nothing but make the best of a bad situation.

'Angela went away, abroad, and she came back with that girl, Gina. Lord alone knows what she promised her; I know that once she got her here she made her life miserable. She couldn't break the girl's spirit, but with her rigid perfectionism, her icy dogmatism, she kept her like a bird in a cage.'

He paused, his thoughts turning inward. I knew he was thinking how best to explain what happened next.

'I felt sorry for her,' he said. 'Alone, so far from home, from everything familiar. But it was more than that. She had spirit. She wasn't afraid to laugh, or cry, or do a little dance step on the lawn if she felt like it. And she turned to me because—I don't know—I suppose I was the only person here who ever had a kind word or a smile for her.'

He looked searchingly at me. 'Can you understand that? We didn't fall in love; we didn't lust after each other. We were drawn together because there was no other human companionship for either of us in this house.'

'I can understand,' I said softly. 'But Angela, what of her? Why didn't she just send Gina away?'

He laughed bitterly. 'Angela? She was in an ecstasy of delight. Do you think she didn't foresee any of that? It was what she had intended all along. It was why she had brought the girl here. She threw us together at every opportunity; she did everything but send the girl to my bed at night.'

'But why?' I asked, surprised.

'It was her particular form of cruelty. She

liked to test people, she said. She would put temptations in their path to see how they would react. If they gave in to the temptation, she could have the joy of forgiving them; if they did not, she found another, greater temptation. She said that the temptations made people stronger, but it was only a game she played. She liked to gloat over people's weaknesses. Throughout all this time, she gloated over the turmoil she was creating for the two of us. She laughed because she knew I was being tempted, and she knew why.

'She grew crueler and crueler to Gina. The poor child didn't understand, didn't know how to cope. Nothing she could do was right, always she was wrong.

'One day I found her in tears. I tried to comfort her. That was all I started out to do, but we were in each other's arms, driven there by a vicious woman using virtue as a whip. I kissed her. That's when Angela came in.'

'The infamous kiss,' I said, shaking my head. 'Mrs. Woodridge made it sound so lurid.'

'It was no more than that, I swear it. But having set this trap for us, Angela was furious now to find us in it. She hadn't anticipated how she herself would react to it. And I made it worse by laughing at her. I told her I didn't want her stupid forgiveness. I had done nothing to be forgiven for. I told her all the things about herself that I've just told you.

'She was livid. She ordered Gina to leave

160

the house that same day. I asked her to show the child a little mercy, but she wouldn't. I mounted my horse and rode into the next town to see if I couldn't make some arrangements for Gina to stay until I could send her back to Italy. I felt we owed her that much.'

He paused again; a log fell on the grate, sending a cascade of sparks upward. 'When I came back, Angela was dead, and Gina was gone. She had run off somewhere. It was storming, and I looked for her for hours but couldn't find her. Mrs. Woodridge told her story of what happened. I couldn't believe it, but there was no one to dispute it. Several days later, Gina was found huddled in a ditch. She had pneumonia. I had her brought back here, but she was out of her head with fever, and she never recovered consciousness.'

'And you blamed yourself for everything that happened,' I said.

'Who else could I blame? I shut up the house, withdrew here. And then, when strange things began to occur, I sent Elizabeth to live with her grandfather. The rest you know.'

'I know that you have spent years punishing yourself for things that weren't your fault,' I said. 'Even if they were, you've been punished enough by now. Angela's gone. However she died, I would say she brought it upon herself. The real tragedy was Gina's.' A thought came to me suddenly. 'Johnathon,' I said, 'when you found Gina in that ditch and brought her back here, who was her nurse?'

'Why, Mrs. Woodridge. There was nobody else, all the other servants left immediately. I had always disliked her, but I thought it was generous of her, under the circumstances, to stay and nurse the sick girl.'

'Perhaps not so generous,' I said. 'We shall never really know whether or not Gina recovered consciousness, shall we? She was the only one who could really dispute Mrs. Woodridge's story.'

'And you think . . .' He paused. 'She'd have been capable of killing the girl to protect Angela's virtuous reputation.'

'Exactly,' I said. 'I would say if anyone has a right to haunt this house, sobbing at night, it is Gina.'

'You're right,' he said, cocking his head as if listening for that ghostly sobbing. The house lay still about us.

'What kind of perfume did Angela wear?' I asked on impulse.

'She would never have worn perfume,' he said. 'She would have considered that wicked.'

'But Gina, with her femininity and her high spirits, surely she must have worn a scent of some sort.'

He shrugged. 'It's been so long ago I hardly remember—yes, I suppose she did, something floral, it seems to me.'

'Gardenias,' I said.

As if summoned by my thoughts, we

162

suddenly heard a faint, distant sound of sobbing. Johnathon got to his feet quickly, but I put out my hand.

'It's all right,' I said. 'She won't harm Elizabeth.'

* * *

I was surprised and not displeased when two days later I received a little note from Isabelle, asking me around to tea. I was looking forward to telling her of my engagement to Johnathon, knowing that she would be quite thrilled, and to bring her up to date on the history of Green Willows and its hauntings.

When I arrived at the appointed time, I found she was not alone. There was a gentleman there, portly and bald but for a few strands of hair that he combed directly across his shiny pate, thus accentuating it.

'I had an idea that you might like meeting Dr. Willoughby,' she said, pouring my tea. 'He was the doctor here when everything was happening at Green Willows. I know you've taken quite an interest in those old happenings.'

She gave me a significant look, intended, I thought, to tell me that she had said nothing to the doctor about the ghostly doings at the house.

'You attended Mrs. Tremayne after her drowning, then?' I asked.

163

'Yes,' he said, nodding his head. 'Not much I could do there, though.'

'Nor apparently in that other death, the Italian girl,' I said tentatively. 'What exactly did she die of? I seem to have forgotten.'

'I put it down as pneumonia,' he said, frowning at his scone.

'Surely, there wasn't any question of that, was there?' I prompted him.

'I wish I could be sure,' he said. 'I've always thought her death was . . . somehow unnecessary. If she'd had better care. Mrs. Tremayne's old nurse was her nurse, and there was undoubtedly some hard feeling.'

'And you think she may have been . . . negligent?' I asked.

'Indifferent would perhaps be closer to the truth,' he said. He sighed and said more firmly, 'It's all so long ago, and who could be sure. At the time, I expected the girl to recover. When she didn't . . . well,' he shrugged, 'maybe I'm just trying to avoid taking the blame.'

'Or maybe there really was negligence,' Isabelle suggested bluntly. 'More tea?'

I waited until he had gone to tell Isabelle my news. She was frankly delighted to learn of the engagement. 'You won't believe this, but I had a hunch from the very first,' she said. 'Oh, Mary, I'm so glad for you. And for Johnathon too. He's needed someone like you all along. And think what it will be for Elizabeth.'

'I'm not so sure that she will welcome the

164

news,' I said. 'She idolizes the memory of her mother. I don't know that she will welcome someone taking her place.'

'But you won't be. You'll just be a second mother, so to speak. She'll come around, mark my word.'

But when I told her what I had learned about Green Willows, Isabelle took a less optimistic view than I. 'I believe it's Gina crying,' I said. 'And it's her gardenia scent that we smell during manifestations.'

Isabelle shook her head. 'No, there's no sense to that. The crying and the gardenias are associated with Elizabeth, and after all, she was Angela's daughter. No matter that husband and wife didn't get along; they aren't the first couple with that complaint, but Angela must have loved her baby. She would be the one coming in to comfort it at night, would she not, and that is what Elizabeth senses now. A stranger would hardly have been doing that. And don't forget, Gina tried to steal the baby. That hints at malevolence and suggests the evil presence you've experienced.'

'It sounds logical,' I admitted, a bit sadly, since my sympathies were all with Gina. 'But in any event, I don't think Elizabeth is in any danger.'

'Maybe, maybe not,' Isabelle said. 'I'd say this—if she ever starts experiencing anything frightening or evil, I'd get her out of there in

165

one big hurry.'

'Perhaps the solution is to get all of us out of there,' I said. 'There've been no definite plans made yet, except that it will have to be done soon. Johnathon thought he would prefer to get married in London and avoid the local gossips.'

'Smart idea,' Isabelle said. 'But you needn't think you'll avoid me. I'm passionate on weddings—someone else's wedding, at least.'

I laughed, promised her that she would be my maid of honor, and started for home. It was late afternoon, a gusty, dark day, and night was already beginning to fall. Green Willows looked somber and unfriendly as I followed the little path around the lake. I fancied that her windows were eyes, watching me, waiting to see what move I would make.

And again I made the wrong one.

CHAPTER EIGHTEEN

Since my return, things at Green Willows had been ominously uneventful. It seemed as if the restless spirits in the house had gone to rest, and I could but wonder if this was good or bad. I had my answer in due time.

In most respects, I was blissfully happy. Did Johnathon not love me, and were we not to be married? We spent long evenings together, talking in low voices of the past, making plans for the future.

Elizabeth was a question mark in our plans, as I was still not certain how she would adjust to having me for a mother. There was only one way to find out, as I said finally to Johnathon, and seizing the next opportunity, I sat her down and attempted to explain.

'You know,' I said, 'that since I came here your father and I have grown quite fond of each other, as I have also grown quite fond of you.'

She made it easier for me by asking, 'Are you in love with him?'

'Yes,' I said frankly. I waited to see how she would take this news.

'Is he in love with you?'

'Yes, he tells me so,' I said.

We were in the schoolroom, and I had taken advantage of a break in our studies to approach the subject. She sat with a history book open on the desk before her, absentmindedly turning its pages back and forth.

'I thought so,' she said, 'from the way you looked at each other. I thought that the first day he brought you to my grandfather's cottage.'

'Then you were a great deal more perceptive than I,' I said with a laugh.

She looked up at me directly. 'Are you going to marry him?'

167

My smile faded, and I said honestly, 'He has asked me to.'

'What did you tell him?'

'I told him that I must first know how you felt about it,' I said.

I held my breath while the moment dragged on. The leaves of the book ruffled to and fro in her hand. At last, she spoke.

'I think you are perfect for each other,' she said, looking up at me with a shy little smile.

'Elizabeth,' I cried, flinging my arms about her and fair squeezing the breath out of her. At last, I stepped back and held her at arm's length. 'But you, will you be happy having me as a member of the family?'

'As my stepmother, you mean? Of course, you have been like a mother to me already. I think if Father had not had the idea I should have suggested it to him myself.'

We both laughed a great deal after that and made a great many silly and sentimental statements, professing our undying affection for each other.

More soberly, I said, 'I shan't try to take your real mother's place, you know.'

'I know,' she said. 'And I wouldn't want you to. But she has been gone since I was a baby. I never really knew her. I never really knew anyone until you came along, except for my grandfather. If it weren't for you, I would still be with him, or I'd be sent away to school somewhere by now. I owe everything to you.'

I reflected silently that that was not necessarily such a good thing; I had learned too much about Green Willows since arguing so ardently that she be allowed to return here. But I did not frighten her with telling what I knew. There would be time enough in her life to learn the truth about her mother. Isabelle was right, nothing I had learned about Angela proved that she did not love her daughter. Indeed, her lingering presence in the house seemed to prove that she did.

A few days later, I was surprised to receive a letter from Brighton. At first, I could not imagine who would be writing to me from there, and I assumed it must be some old friend of my aunt's.

The handwriting was completely unfamiliar. I glanced at it and turned the letter over to see the signature.

'Why, it's from Mrs. Woodridge,' I said to Johnathon.

'That old witch? What can she possibly want?' he asked, putting aside the book he had been reading.

'She wants Elizabeth,' I said, reading rapidly. 'She says it is what Angela would have wanted. Here, listen to this: "Angela will never rest happily until the child is delivered to my care. You owe it to the child and to Angela to persuade her father to agree to this." Can you imagine, I owe it to Angela.'

'That old crone will never get her hands on

Elizabeth, not so long as I'm alive to prevent it,' Johnathon said vehemently. 'Not even if Angela brings the house down about our ears.'

I thought of Mrs. Woodridge's School of Angela's Kindness, and I could not but be grateful for Johnathon's attitude, but I was not altogether sure Angela might not do just what he suggested.

Still the ghosts were silent. They were only biding their time, of course, lulling us into a false sense of tranquillity so that when something occurred again it would be twice as unnerving. But at the time, we fell into the trap and even began to congratulate ourselves that perhaps Angela had given up.

'Maybe because we're in love,' Johnathon said. 'Maybe that convinced her how hopeless her case is.'

*   *   *

I woke one night shivering with the cold. At first, wrapped tightly in my covers, I thought that my fire had gone out, but I gradually became aware of the shadows on my walls as the flames danced and leaped on the hearth. The fire was still burning. This was no normal cold but that same intense, unnatural chill that I had experienced before with that terrifying apparition.

I sat up, my heart pounding, clutching the blankets about me. The room was empty, despite the cold.

Suddenly, a scream rent the air.

'Elizabeth,' I said in a hoarse whisper and clambered from my bed, fumbling in the half light for my robe and slippers.

The hall was in darkness. I hesitated for a second at the top of the stairs, half expecting to see that eerie mist again, but there was nothing. Behind me, I heard soft footsteps. I turned, and Johnathon came up beside me.

'Not you, then,' he said breathlessly. 'But who?'

'Elizabeth,' I said.

'Stay here,' he said, starting past me.

'No,' I replied and ran after him. He did not argue with me, knowing no doubt that it would only waste time and breath.

I had enough presence of mind to realize as we went that the icy cold was not here, nor was there any smell of gardenias.

We found Elizabeth huddled in one corner of her bed, pressed against the wall. The door to the outside was again open, and a cold wind was blowing through the room, but it was a natural, nighttime cold. I closed the door while Johnathon took his daughter in his arms.

'What is it?' he asked. 'What happened?'

For a moment, she could only cling to him, shivering. I lit a lamp, its soft glow diffusing the room's hovering shadows.

'It must have been a nightmare,' she said at last through chattering teeth. 'I'm sorry.'

'What was it like?' I asked.

'I don't know exactly—I woke up, or thought I did, and the room was so cold. There was this . . . I don't know what to call it, a mist, like a greenish fog, and glowing; it filled the room, and I thought, from the very center of it, I saw two eyes watching me. I was terrified. I can't explain any better than that. I closed my eyes and screamed—and then you two were here.'

She pressed her face against her father's chest. He and I exchanged frightened glances. Whatever the evil in the house, whatever its purpose, the situation had now changed; it was now threatening Elizabeth just as Isabelle had predicted. And for that, there was only one solution—for her own sake, we must remove her from Green Willows.

She looked up at us, from Johnathon's worried face to mine. 'It was just a dream, wasn't it?' she asked anxiously.

Johnathon looked helplessly at me.

'Perhaps not,' I said slowly. 'Perhaps it is time you knew the truth.'

CHAPTER NINETEEN

Mrs. Duffy came in just then, frightened by the disturbance.

'Elizabeth has had a nightmare,' I said.

172

'Perhaps you would be so good as to fix us all some hot chocolate; I think we could all use a little something.'

'To be sure, miss,' she said, giving me a sideways look. She hurried off to do as I had asked, and in a short time, we were ensconced before the fire in the study, sipping warm mugs of steaming chocolate.

It was I who explained the hauntings to Elizabeth. I told her all we knew about the presence of spirits in the house. I did not see fit to tell her the truth about her mother's character; I thought that would be rather too much for her to absorb at one sitting.

She took the news that Green Willows was haunted rather calmly. 'I wondered,' she said. 'So many strange things happening.'

'I'm glad you've taken it so well,' I said, relieved to have at least part of the truth out in the open. 'I was afraid you might resist leaving Green Willows and then . . .'

'Leave Green Willows?' she cried aghast, leaping to her feet. 'But what on earth for?'

'But I've just explained,' I said, bewildered. 'The hauntings . . .'

'But I'm not afraid of that,' she said, dismissing them with a gesture. 'Don't you see, it's my mother, looking for me, longing to be with me after all these years of being separated from me. She wouldn't harm me. She only wants to be with me.'

'But tonight you were terrified,' Johnathon

said. 'You screamed when you saw her.'

'I was half asleep, that's all,' she said. 'And I didn't understand then. I didn't know who it was. But now that I know, I'll never be frightened again. How could I be frightened of my own dear mother.'

She turned on me and said accusingly, 'You should have told me before. You should have told me from the start.'

'Elizabeth,' Johnathon said, speaking slowly and firmly. 'I can understand how you must feel, but the fact remains that there is danger here, and I cannot permit you to be exposed to it further. You will do as I tell you; I will make arrangements tomorrow for you to leave Green Willows, and as soon as possible, the three of us will be together someplace else.'

'I won't go,' she screamed, her face suddenly twisted with rage. 'You can't make me go. You've kept me from her all these years because you hated her, but you won't take me from her again.'

'Elizabeth,' I cried, shocked by the ugliness of her mood.

'It's true,' she said turning to me. 'He killed her, you know. That's why he's locked himself away in this house all these years; that's why he tried to make me forget all about her. But I won't, and she hasn't forgotten either. All this time, she's waited here for me to come to her, and now that I have, I won't leave. I won't! I won't! I won't!'

174

She ran from the room, sobbing. We heard her steps in the hall and then the sound of her door being slammed.

Johnathon's face was ashen. I put a hand on his shoulder. 'She's overwrought,' I said. 'A bad dream, then the news that her mother's spirit is haunting the house. She'll be calmer in the morning and more reasonable, I'm sure.'

He patted my hand and said gently, 'It's late. You'd better go back to bed.'

As I was leaving the room, though, he said one thing that kept me awake most of the remainder of the night.

'She sounded exactly like Angela just then.'

*   *   *

It was at this critical juncture that Commander Whittsett suddenly stepped into the picture again. It had been better for him, for all of us, had he not done so, but how was he to know that his well-meaning efforts would only bring down further tragedy?

He arrived early the following afternoon, quite unannounced. Elizabeth had not budged from her room and had spoken so rudely to both Johnathon and me that he had responded by sending her to the schoolroom with orders to remain there until he told her otherwise.

'At least we will know where she is and that she is in no danger,' he said to me.

It was then that the commander arrived.

Mrs. Duffy barely had time to hurry into the parlor and announce him before the old man was there, close on her heels.

'Commander,' I greeted him, trying to ignore his frosty look. 'How good to see you again.'

'No doubt,' he said, nodding at his former son-in-law. 'No doubt. So you think you'll be mistress of this godforsaken place, do you?'

'You've heard then,' I said, hardly surprised. News such as an engagement was not long in being spread in such a small village; no doubt Mrs. Duffy had wasted no time gossiping. 'I hope you'll wish me well.'

'There's nothing good can come to anyone in this house,' he said. 'Nor with Johnathon Tremayne as a husband.'

'Thank you for your confidence,' Johnathon said smoothly, making a little bow from the waist. 'What can we do for you, Commander, since it seems you did not come to offer your felicitations?'

'I've come for the girl,' he said.

Johnathon sighed and said, 'We've been all through that before.'

'Aye, that we have,' the commander said. 'But this time you'll not be putting me off. I've come for her, and I mean to take her with me when I leave.'

'As a matter of fact,' Johnathon said, remaining unperturbed, 'it is my plan that Elizabeth leave Green Willows, but I do not

176

intend to return her to your cottage. She will be staying with friends until Mary and I are married, after which the three of us will make a journey abroad.'

'Journey all you want, with whomever you want,' the commander said. 'But Elizabeth will not be going with you. I've already written this morning to Mrs. Woodridge, telling her to enroll Elizabeth as a pupil in her school.'

'Mrs. Woodridge.' I gasped. 'Her school in Brighton? But why?'

'Why?' he said, taking a letter from his pocket. 'Do I have to tell you why? Because of the things that have been going on in this house, that's why. I listened to the stories spread by your own housekeeper, and I kept my tongue. But this, if I'm to believe what I'm told, comes direct from you, Miss Uppity.'

He thrust the letter at me. I took it, recognizing Mrs. Woodridge's bold, rigid handwriting. My hands trembled slightly as I removed the letter from its envelope.

She must have written to him immediately after I had left her office, for the letter contained nearly a verbatim account of our conversation, including my statement to the effect that Angela's spirit was haunting Green Willows.

I handed it to Johnathon, who scanned it quickly and handed it back to the old man.

'If you try to fight me on this,' the commander said, 'I'll give this to my solicitor.

177

I'll bring this whole spooky business before the bench if I have to, but I'll not have that girl living here with hauntings and ghosts and God alone knows what else going on.'

'I doubt that the bench would place much importance on ghost stories,' Johnathon said. 'And I am the child's father.'

'Commander,' I said. 'I've been to Mrs. Woodridge's school. It's an awful place. I believe sending a girl there would be condemning her to unhappiness.'

'She was my daughter's nurse and companion,' he said. 'And she did a fine job by her. Better, I dare say, than you've done by Elizabeth. Where is the girl? I want to talk to her?'

'If you think it will change anything, you're welcome to do so,' Johnathon said. 'She's in the schoolroom. Shall I take you there?'

'I know the way,' he said, and whirling about, he left the room. We heard his measured tread on the stairs.

'Talk about the horns of a dilemma,' Johnathon said. 'She refuses to leave for us, and he insists on taking her away with him.'

He was upstairs perhaps twenty minutes. Twice we heard his voice raised argumentatively, and Johnathon half rose from his chair to go up.

'No, let them be,' I cautioned. 'Perhaps she will convince her grandfather for us. Then we'll only have one of them to contend with.'

178

Silence descended. Whatever was being discussed was said in a lower voice. Suddenly, a door crashed open, and the commander's voice could be clearly heard.

'I will have my way in this,' he roared. 'Come hell or high water.'

We did not hear Elizabeth's reply, if any. The commander's footsteps could be heard resounding along the hall. He reached the stairs . . . there was a pause . . . and suddenly, a cry, and the sound of someone falling down the stairs.

'Merciful heavens,' I cried, leaping to my feet.

Johnathon was ahead of me, rushing into the hall. I followed and stopped in my tracks. The commander lay in a crumpled heap at the foot of the stairs. Johnathon ran to him and knelt over him.

'Is he . . . ?' I asked, coming up.

'Dead,' Johnathon said, staring up at me, horror struck.

'Oh,' I gasped, putting a hand to my mouth to stifle a scream. My first thought was of Eleanor and the mysterious accident that had sent her wheelchair plummeting over the cliff to her death.

'He must have tripped as he started down,' Johnathon said.

'Johnathon,' I said, 'what if he didn't trip? What if he were . . . were shoved?'

'Good heavens, by whom?' Johnathon

demanded. 'Surely, you don't think . . .'

'By Angela,' I whispered, honor making my voice drop. 'To prevent his taking Elizabeth.'

'By . . .' He stopped incredulous; but he considered it, I saw that it became less incredible to him. 'But would Angela try to stop him from taking Elizabeth to Mrs. Woodridge?'

'Then by Gina,' I cried. 'Perhaps Isabelle is right. Perhaps Gina is the evil force here. Or . . . oh, Johnathon.'

'What?' He stood, taking my hands in his own. 'What is it?'

'Perhaps they—whoever is here—doesn't want Elizabeth to leave—ever.'

CHAPTER TWENTY

'What is it?' Elizabeth called from above. 'What was all that racket? It sounded like someone . . . ?'

She stopped halfway down the stairs, staring at us. Johnathon and I had froze in place, unable to think how to answer her.

'Grandfather,' she shrieked and flew down the stairs to fling herself upon his body. 'What have they done to you?'

I shall never quite be sure who she meant by 'they.'

*　　　*　　　*

Mrs. Duffy announced that she was leaving. It took all our combined powers of persuasion to coax her to stay on a few more days.

'As soon as I am able to arrange quarters for us, we shall all be leaving,' Johnathon said, adding, when she had gone, 'And I hope I never see this cursed place again.'

Mrs. Duffy agreed to stay out the week, by which time Johnathon felt we would surely be on our way. The services for the commander were held the following day; he had no remaining relatives except his granddaughter. We went, and Isabelle came and stood with us during the services. The townspeople turned out almost to a man; they stood in a wide semicircle beyond the grave and stared at us throughout.

Elizabeth felt her grandfather's death keenly. She was subdued and polite and offered no further arguments about our plans.

We had decided that we would leave on Friday. It was our plan to journey to London, where we would be married, and from there to travel on to the continent. Johnathon had suggested that his solicitor handle the matter of my aunt's home, which I had decided to dispose of. The question still remained where we would live when we returned from our travels; certainly, we would not be returning to Green Willows, but neither did I fancy

181

Brighton.

'Perhaps some place near here,' I said. 'I've come to like the area, and it is Elizabeth's home.'

I was relieved when the funeral was over. I knew that the rumors about Green Willows and about us were being spawned anew with the commander's sudden death, and I did not flatter myself that the curiosity everyone was showing was especially friendly.

When we had returned to the house, Johnathon drew me aside. 'I'll have to go into town to look after the commander's affairs.'

'Will you be back by evening?' I asked, glancing toward the window. It looked as if a storm were brewing.

'I'll try. Stay with Elizabeth, won't you?' I promised that she would be safe with me, and he kissed me and rode toward town.

Mrs. Duffy was just serving our dinner when someone knocked at the front door. Johnathon was not yet home, and thinking it might be some message from him, I hurried to the door myself.

It was a moment before I recognized the cloaked figure as the little half-wit girl who worked at the local tavern for Mrs. Jenkins.

'What can I do for you?' I asked, bringing her into the hall and away from the wind that was blowing up outside.

'Mrs. Jenkins, she said for you to come,' the girl said, wagging her finger in front of my

182

nose for emphasis. 'She say she got to talk to you, right away.'

'But, really, I can't go out now,' I said, thinking of the approaching storm and of Elizabeth. 'Tell Mrs. Jenkins I'll try to see her tomorrow.'

She wagged the finger again. 'She say, tell you to come right off. She's going to tell you all about what happened. She say she know the truth, and nobody else does.'

'The truth about what?' I asked.

'She say she the only one knows what really happened up here that night, the night the Angel-lady died.'

That was all the coaxing I needed, of course. The storm was not yet too close, and it was not a long walk into town. Johnathon would be home shortly, and in any event, there was Mrs. Duffy, who could surely be trusted.

'Wait,' I said to the girl and went in search of Mrs. Duffy. 'I've got to go out,' I told her. 'I want you to stay with Miss Elizabeth.'

'Surely, miss,' she said, putting aside the work she was doing.

'You understand, you are not to let her out of your sight. That's important.'

'I do understand, miss,' she said emphatically.

Confident that I had left Elizabeth in capable hands, I threw a cloak about my shoulders and started off with the girl from the tavern. I started instinctively for the path that

183

circled the lake, but she stopped me.

'This way,' she said. She led me to another path that went along the very edge of the cliffs and directly into town. It was much shorter, although it would, I guessed, be treacherous on a dark and stormy night.

We were there in less than half an hour. I had questioned in my mind the propriety of showing up at the tavern, but my hostess had thought of this before me; I was led about to the back door and ushered into her kitchen. It was bright and warm and scented with cooking things. In the distance, I could hear the sounds from the taproom, men singing and talking, some arguing, the clink of glasses, and smoke mingled with the kitchen smells.

The girl signaled to a chair before the old iron stove and disappeared through a door; the bar noises rose for a moment, then died again as the door swung closed.

'I'm glad you could come,' Mrs. Jenkins said, coming through the door a moment later.

'I can't stay,' I said. 'I have to get back.'

'I understand,' she said, but she seemed in no hurry. She poured herself a cup of tea from a huge pot and offered me some, but I declined.

'A lot of people wouldn't have come at all,' she said. 'But then I wouldn't have sent for anybody else, I expect.'

'Your girl said you could tell me the story of what happened up at Green Willows,' I said to prompt her. 'I think if I knew that I would know better how to cope with present problems.'

'You're planning on giving up the house, I hear,' she said. 'Oh, don't look surprised. This town thrives on gossip.'

She seated herself in a chair facing mine. I heard distant laughter and, closer at hand, the ticking of a clock on the mantel.

'Mrs. Jenkins,' I began.

'You were nice to me,' she said. 'And I know you care about the little girl. Else I wouldn't have sent for you. I wanted to tell you about that girl, the one they used to have up at the house.'

'Gina' I asked, my flagging interest reviving.

'That's the one,' she said. 'People around here talk about her, call her foreign and crazy, say she murdered Mrs. Tremayne. I'm here to tell you none of it was true. She wouldn't have harmed a fly. You can take it from me.'

'Somehow I thought that myself,' I said.

'It was that other one, the one everyone called an angel—ha! She was a devil if ever there was one. I used to talk to Gina. I suppose I was the only friend she had around here. She was Italian, you know, same as my first husband, and she couldn't talk any English, but I knew a little Italian, and she used to slip down here when the missus didn't know about it, and we'd talk.' She paused, staring at the glow of the fire through the

185

windowed door.

'What sort of things did she talk about?' I asked.

'About how unhappy she was, mostly. She was like a duck out of water here. No one understood her. She was lonesome, so lonesome she would cry over it. If it hadn't been for him—Mr. Tremayne, I mean, she liked him—and that baby, why, I don't know how she'd have stood it as long as she did.'

'Was she fond of little Elizabeth?' I asked.

'Like it was her own baby,' she said. 'And that other one, that Angela, she was so mean. Gina used to cry on my shoulder not just because of the way Angela treated her but because of the way she treated her husband, and especially the baby.'

'Angela was cruel to her baby too?' I asked. 'In what way?'

'Lots of little ways,' she said. 'Like, the little one used to be afraid of the dark, and she wanted a light in her room, but Angela wouldn't have that. She said that that was coddling her, and she wouldn't let Gina sleep with the baby either. But Gina used to steal down to the nursery anyway with a light and comfort the little one. Of course, whenever Mrs. Tremayne or that nurse caught her, why there'd be the devil to pay.'

'Then it wasn't her mother she remembers,' I said thoughtfully. 'It was Gina all along. Tell me something, did Gina used to hum a song

186

. . . wait, let me think how it goes.'

It came to me in a minute, and I hummed a snatch of the song I had heard at Green Willows, the one Elizabeth thought her mother used to hum.

'That was Gina's song,' she said, looking beyond me into the past. 'An old Italian folk song, wait a minute, let me think how it goes . . .' She sang a snatch of the song in Italian, the words fluid and soft.

'And Gina wore gardenia perfume,' I said.

'All the time, it was her one luxury. Angela Tremayne forbade it. She disapproved of perfume, but Gina kept hers hidden, and she could never find it. She constantly berated her for wearing it, but Gina persisted.'

'Gina,' I said. 'It was always Gina. She is the one Elizabeth remembers, the one who cared for her, the one who loved her. Angela Tremayne was no more a mother than she was a wife. She was a sham, pretending to be an angel, a saint, and all the while she was incapable of love, incapable of any kindness. She took her pleasure in torturing people, making them suffer—even her daughter had to lie in fear of the night to satisfy her cruel idea of virtue.'

Mrs. Jenkins smiled in an oddly triumphant way. I suppose because at last, if only with one person, she was able to vindicate that maligned peasant girl.

'Tell me,' I said, leaning forward in my

187

chair, 'what really happened that night at Green Willows?'

'There was an ugly quarrel,' she said. 'Angela had struck Gina because she found her rocking the baby and singing to her; Angela called that coddling the child. She slapped Gina, and Gina ran from her. Mr. Tremayne found her crying and tried to comfort her, and his wife found them together. She ordered Gina to leave the house at once.

'The child was terrified. She didn't know what she was to do or where she was to go. And he left. Mr. Tremayne rode away on his horse.'

'He was trying to find a place for her to stay until he could send her back to Italy,' I said.

'I didn't know that. Neither did she. She thought she had been completely abandoned. She was hysterical, mind you. She did try to take the baby, as the story was, not to steal her; she meant somehow to shield the child from her mother's cruelty. I don't suppose she was thinking very clearly. Anyway, Angela found her, and they fought. Again Gina ran from her—she didn't know how to cope with that sort of cruelty. But Angela must have been half crazy by then too. She chased her and caught up with her by the lake, and she tried to throw Gina into the water.'

'So that's the truth of that,' I murmured.

'I suppose she meant to drown her, knowing she couldn't swim. But it was Angela who fell

188

into the lake. Gina tried to save her, but Angela fought her off. Panic, I suppose. She drowned while Gina tried to save her, and suddenly the old dragon, Mrs. Woodridge, was there, screaming at Gina, accusing her of murdering Angela.'

'But how do you know all this?' I asked. 'I understood Gina caught pneumonia and died without ever recovering consciousness.'

'She came here when she ran away from Green Willows,' Mrs. Jenkins said. 'She was half drowned and already running a fever, not to mention terrified out of her mind. I took her in, listened to her story, and put her to bed.'

'But how did she come to be found lying in a ditch days later?' I asked.

'She ran away from here. They were looking for her. I had gone out, and someone came around asking questions. I suppose she must have thought she would get me into trouble. When I came back, she was gone. The next I heard of her, they'd found her out of her head with pneumonia.'

I was thoughtful for a moment, looking back upon that tragic chain of events. Yet it seemed to me that the most tragic part of all was that the truth had never come out, and Gina, the real victim of the story, had been maligned all these years.

'Why didn't you tell this before?' I asked.

She shrugged and said, 'To whom? No one

189

would have listened to me; no one would have believed me. They all hated Gina because she was foreign, and they worshipped Angela as a saint.'

'I suppose you're right,' I admitted reluctantly.

'I have a business to run,' she went on, excusing herself perhaps more to herself than to me. 'They'd have run me out of business, out of town even. No one would have believed me.'

'And yet,' I said, 'I did, without question.'

She stared sullenly back at me, no doubt regretting the impulse that had led her to share her story after so many years.

'I thought you'd understand,' she said. 'You were different, always friendly like, talking to me when lots of others wouldn't. I thought you'd want to know.'

'Yes, I did,' I said, rising. 'And I thank you for telling me. Now I'd better get back to Green Willows.'

Lightning flashed as I opened the door. She had come to the door with me, and she glanced up at the blackened sky.

'Take the cliff path,' she said. 'It's faster, and you'll get home before the storm breaks.'

When she had gone in, though, and the door was closed upon her, I hesitated for a moment in the darkness. I did not relish walking an unfamiliar path in the dark and in a storm.

Yet something impelled me to hurry, some sixth sense that suddenly warned of danger. With an anxious glance at the sky, I began to follow the path along the cliffs.

CHAPTER TWENTY-ONE

I walked quickly and with a new confidence in my step. At last, I knew the truth about Angela and the events at Green Willows, and the truth was a powerful weapon. I need no longer be afraid of Angela's presence in the house; she was a sham, a fake, and she always had been. She did not come back to find her daughter or to look after her. She came back to do what she had done all her life, to torment, to torture, to frighten, and to hurt.

It was Gina who cried at night and hummed, who hovered near Elizabeth and tried to look after her, who had always loved her as if she were her own.

'Your frightening days are numbered, Angela,' I whispered as I neared the house. I had made excellent time despite the necessity for watching my step carefully on the strange and treacherous path.

This path brought me along the headlands; from here, I saw the rear of the house, the sloping lawn that ran down to the cliff, and the one twisted tree that guarded its edge. From this angle, Green Willows looked macabre and uninviting, and I could well understand how people would be afraid and invent stories.

The storm was threatening in earnest now, with great jagged bolts of lightning ripping across the black sky, to be followed by crashes and sonorous rumbles of thunder. A few drops of rain fell tentatively, like advance guards; then, as suddenly as if a bucket had been emptied over a rail, the rain began to pour down.

In a twinkling, I could see nothing but the great sheets of water driving down, whipped into my face by the wind. I grasped my cloak tightly about me and leaned forward against the wind. The path this way was indeed shorter, but I was exposed to all the wind from the sea, and it was like hands clutching at me, holding me back. The night was inky and impenetrable except when the flashes of lightning lighted the scene with their eerie glow. Then I saw the house, the tree, the cliff, like grim sets for some horror play, unreal looking and yet real in the sense of the desolation they lent.

At last, I was almost there, and already the bulk of the house somewhat hindered the rush of the wind, and I could move more quickly. I was drenched and chilled to the bone, but for all that, my trip into town had left me with a sense of triumph. This house and its haunting presence still had the power to frighten but not to overpower me; knowledge gave me strength. I knew Angela Tremayne for the cruel, heartless sham she was. In life and in death, she might overpower Gina, but I was made of stronger stuff, and I would not again be intimidated as I was before.

Something moved from the rear of the house, a ghostly white flutter. I stopped, wondering if my very thoughts had carried to the house, had roused the spirit of Angela. Was she come to meet me, to challenge my new courage? Let her come then. I would meet her here if I must, in the rain and the wind and the dark, meet her and bring her down.

The lightning flashed, and for an instant, the stage was lighted with blue white light. In that flash, I saw the movement again, and my heart leaped within me.

It was Elizabeth, in her nightdress, running. Running for the cliff!

'Elizabeth!' I screamed, but the light had vanished, the darkness rushing in upon its wake, and no answering call came on the wind. I vaguely saw that flutter of white, still rushing down the slope.

I was closer to the cliff, and the path went along at an angle that eventually intercepted her route, but I was so far away from that point that it seemed I could never reach her.

'Elizabeth, wait!' I screamed and began to run. I knew even as I screamed that it was futile, that she could not, or would not hear, that she was beyond hearing. I had felt that overpowering presence. I knew how it could cloud the mind, defeat reason. If only for a moment, it had urged me toward self-destruction, as I knew it was now urging Elizabeth. That she was out of her mind, out of control, I knew; nothing I could call, nothing I could do short of physically stopping her would dissuade her from that self-destructive race to the cliff's edge.

Yet I screamed again as I ran. It seemed as if my feet were leaded, as if each gust of wind conspired with Angela to hold me back, to slow my race. The wind tore my cloak from my head, and my hair blew about my face. I could hardly see until another flaring burst of light showed me Elizabeth, still running crazily downward. She slipped in the mud and fell, and for a moment, I dared to hope. But even before the light vanished, I saw her scramble to her feet, her dress filthy with mud and rain, and begin to run again.

My lungs were afire with the effort of dragging air into them; my movements seemed too slow. I must reach her in time, and yet I could not.

I stepped in water, a deep puddle, and my foot slipped. In a moment, I had fallen forward, landing in mud. I threw my hands out to break my fall and scrambled at once to my feet again, but surely, the fall had lost me the race.

'Mrs. Duffy,' I shrieked at the top of my lungs.

Where was she? Why was she not with Elizabeth? How had Elizabeth escaped her like this?

I was too late. She had already passed the point where our routes would have intercepted and was on that last, steep-pitched slant to the edge. I veered to the right, not daring to think that on this grade, running like this in the mud and rain, I would never be able to stop myself before I pitched over the cliff. I saw two things in the next lightning flash, and two things only: Elizabeth and the gnarled tree that stood only inches from the edge.

I was running behind her now, too exhausted and out of breath even to try to call her name. Somewhere far away, through the crash of thunder, I heard Johnathon call my name, but I dared not stop, dared not even pause.

Closer, closer . . . I stretched, reaching, reaching, my fingers working frantically. The wet cloth of her dress brushed the tips of my fingers, tantalizing and yet still not enough. Ahead of us yawned the empty blackness beyond the edge, but now it seemed no longer empty. It seemed to be peopled with a multitude of spirits, phantom shapes, mocking voices, whispering winds.

I gave one last, drawn-out cry—'Elizabeth!'

The wind snatched it from my lips, flinging it behind me. My fingers caught in her dress . . . and held.

I could not stop. I had her arm now, held in a grip I would never have dreamed I possessed, but our momentum was too much, the pitch downward too steep. She dragged me along, and my feet slipped again. We fell, rolling and sliding in the mud. Three yards, rolling, tumbling, sliding, trying to stop our descent—two yards, the wind ripping and rushing, the thunder a drumroll crescendo to our doom—a yard, the emptiness before me, the lightning showing me wind-whipped waves, white with frenzy, far below. I kicked and clawed, trying to find some handhold, some way to break our plunge.

I caught the tree, the knobby branch that hung low. It bent, creaked—and held. My arm felt as if it were being jerked out of its socket, but my fingers would not unclench.

Everything stopped. The cessation of movement was like a shock after that insane race. I was surprised to discover, with one part of my consciousness, that I was crying, the tears mingling with the rain that ran down my face. My body shook and heaved with my sobs and labored breath.

Elizabeth lay motionless and still. She had fainted or had been knocked unconscious when we fell. I could be grateful at least that she was not struggling in my grip, for my aching hand could not have held her if she was. But it was little enough to be grateful for. Any second now, she would slip from my grasp anyway. I could not pull her back from the edge, where she dangled half on land, half suspended in the air. I could not release my grip on the tree to get a better hold on her. I could only lay there in the mud and the water, clinging desperately to our precarious perch, and pray.

I had all but forgotten Johnathon, calling behind me, but suddenly, he was there, his strong hands reaching for me.

'Don't move,' he said, crouching over me.

'Elizabeth,' I tried to say, but my voice came out the croaking of a frog.

'I'll get her. Can you hold on?'

'I think so,' I managed to whisper.

He slid down, taking his daughter into his arms, lifting her. Relieved of that burden, I could grasp the tree more securely with both hands. I clung there, dizzy with weariness, until in a moment he had come back for me.

I could have stood with his help, but instead, he lifted me in his arms as he had done with Elizabeth and carried me back up the hill toward Green Willows. He put me down in the wet grass beside Elizabeth.

'I'll have to carry her in,' he said, kneeling above me. Never had his face looked so handsome to me as it did then, with his concern a revelation in it. 'Will you be all right

197

here till I come back?'

'When I get my breath back, I'll walk in,' I said.

'No. Stay here.' He took off his jacket and put it about my shoulders. He leaned closer and kissed me briefly, his lips the brush of a butterfly's wings upon mine. Then he was gone. In a burst of light, I saw him running toward the house, Elizabeth in his arms.

Perhaps I fainted briefly; it seemed a moment, no more, before he returned, again taking me up in his arms. I lay against the warm strength of his chest, glad for once to feel little and helpless and cared for.

CHAPTER TWENTY-TWO

Later, safe in my bed, I remembered to ask about Mrs. Duffy. 'I left her with Elizabeth,' I said. 'Is she all right?'

'She is now,' Johnathon said. 'I came back and found her with Elizabeth and you out. The storm was threatening, so I rode out to look for you along the path.'

'I came by the cliff path,' I said.

'When I didn't find you, I came back here and found Mrs. Duffy unconscious on the floor and Elizabeth missing. The door from her bedroom was open, and I came outside in time to see you trying to catch her. I thought I had lost you both.'

I sighed wearily and said, 'For a few minutes, I thought so myself.'

The next morning, Mrs. Duffy remembered nothing of what had happened. 'All I know is that I got awfully cold,' she said. 'And then the next thing, I'm lying on the sofa and Mr. Tremayne is trying to get some brandy down my throat.'

Nothing, however, could persuade her to stay any longer. 'I mean to pack my bags and be gone by sundown,' she said flatly.

'So shall we all be,' Johnathon said. 'I'm taking Elizabeth over to Isabelle Simpson's for the duration. I'll find a place for you somewhere,' he told me. 'I can always get a room at the tavern myself.'

'I'm sure Isabelle will put Elizabeth and I both up for the night,' I said.

Isabelle, as it turned out, was delighted. 'You might have to curl up with the paint pots,' she said. 'But never mind that. You'll be warm anyway.'

We left Elizabeth with her and returned to Green Willows to pack. 'I'd have been more at ease if you had stayed the day with Isabelle too,' Johnathon said, but I would not hear of it.

'You needn't worry about me,' I told him. 'I'm not afraid of Angela anymore. As a matter of fact, I rather hope she does show up again. There are a few things I'd like to say to her.'

As it turned out, I was to have my chance to speak my mind to Angela, but not quite as I had anticipated.

It took most of the day to pack. We were without servants; they had all left already, and Johnathon's efforts to find help for the day met with no success.

'I'm quite used to doing for myself,' I assured him. 'It's only a matter of packing my things and Elizabeth's. Everything else can remain until we return.'

'Or forever,' he said bitterly, looking around. 'I don't care if I never see this place again.'

It was a prophetic remark, although we did not know so at the time.

Morning became afternoon, and afternoon moved on toward evening. As the shadows lengthened, I began to have an eerie feeling of being watched. Johnathon was outside at the time, preparing the carriage and feeding and watering the horses; yet I felt distinctly that I was not alone in the house. Once or twice I glanced over my shoulder apprehensively, expecting to see someone—or something—but there was nothing there.

At last, my things were packed, as well as Johnathon's and Elizabeth's. I looked around wondering if there were anything in particular that should be taken with us from Green Willows. It came to me suddenly that I had never done something Elizabeth had asked me to do. I had never given her anything of her mother's. Someday I would have to explain to her the truth about her mother, and that it was really an Italian peasant girl that she remembered so lovingly; for now, though, I thought it might make the move easier for her if I found some special souvenir she could carry with her.

I knew now where Mrs. Duffy kept the keys, and fetching them from the kitchen, I made my way up the stairs and to the room that had been Angela's.

I had not needed the keys after all. To my surprise, the door was unlocked. The knob turned easily in my hand, and as it did so, I heard a quick, rustling movement from within as though someone, or something, scurried from sight.

I held my breath and pushed the door inward. The air in the room was musty and stale. I could see no one, but the draperies were closed, making the room dark and gloomy.

I stepped inside. 'Angela?' I whispered.

Something moved behind me, and the door suddenly slammed closed. I squealed and whirled about—and found myself face to face with Elizabeth.

'Elizabeth, what on earth?' I cried, my fright making me angry. 'What are you doing here? Why aren't you at Isabelle's, where we left you?'

'I snuck out,' she said, giggling. 'I had to come back. Gosh, if you had only seen yourself.'

'You gave me quite a fright, young lady,' I said, breathing more easily. 'I think you'd better come downstairs with me and explain to your father.'

She made a face, but she came willingly enough with me. Johnathon was just coming in as we descended the stairs.

'Elizabeth,' he said, surprised to see her. 'What are you doing here?'

'She slipped out of Isabelle's and came back to say good-bye to the place,' I explained.

'I won't say good-bye,' Elizabeth said. 'This is my home. Why do you want to force me to leave it against my will?'

'We've been all through this,' Johnathon said. 'You know I didn't want you here today at all. Last night you nearly killed yourself, and Mary too.'

'I don't remember,' she said sullenly. 'How do I know you haven't made that up?'

This remark was so patently rude that Johnathon was left speechless. All he could finally say was, 'I'll discuss that with you later, young lady. For now, I think it's time we were all leaving. The carriage is ready, Mary.'

'Johnathon,' I said softly. For a moment, I had hardly heard anything that was said. 'Have you noticed how cold it's gotten?'

'Why, now that you mention it . . .' He suddenly realized the significance of my question and gave me a startled look. 'We'd better go,' he said, taking Elizabeth's arm.

'Look,' I said, pointing.

The stairs were between us and the front door. A grayish-green mist had begun to form at the bottom of the stairs, blocking our path.

'Is that . . . ?' he started to ask.

'Yes,' I said grimly. 'It's her. She's going to try to stop us.'

'Come on,' Johnathon said, taking my arm as well and propelling me forward.

'No,' I said. 'Not that way. Take Elizabeth and go out the back way. . .'

'I won't go,' Elizabeth said sharply.

'You'll do as you're told,' Johnathon said.

'I won't, she cried, jerking her arm free of his grasp. 'You can't make me any more than the others could.'

'What are you talking about?' he demanded. 'What others?'

'Aunt Eleanor,' she said, backing away from him and pressing the palms of her hands flat against the wall. 'And Grandfather. They tried to make me leave here too, but they couldn't, and neither can you. No one can take me from my mother again.'

Her eyes flashed wildly, and her voice had risen on an hysterical note. 'Elizabeth,' I said, a new horror creeping unbidden into my mind. 'What do you mean about Aunt Eleanor and your grandfather?'

She narrowed her eyes, and her face suddenly took on a look of cunning. 'She tried to make Father send me away. I went to her and begged her to let me stay, and she only said I couldn't stay in this house. And then that day I saw her outside on the back lawn, and I knew how to handle her. So I offered to push her chair for her, and I got it going faster and faster, and she started crying and saying that I could stay, that she'd talk to my father, and then I gave the chair a hard shove, and let go of it.'

'Oh, my God,' Johnathon gasped, staring in horror at his daughter.

'And your grandfather?' I persisted. I was virtually reeling from the shock and had to put my hand out to steady myself. 'You pushed him too, didn't you?'

'He said he was going to take me away,' she said, a sullen note creeping into her voice. 'I said I wanted to stay, but he yelled at me and told me it wasn't up to me. He said he'd take me away from here if it was the last thing he did, and then he walked away from me. I saw him on the stairs, and I thought, it's the only way. So I ran up to him and pushed . . . He rolled over and over and over, all the way to the bottom.'

An involuntary groan escaped Johnathon's lips. 'What have I done?' he asked.

'Johnathon,' I said and touched his arm. He

followed the direction of my gaze.

We had been so absorbed in Elizabeth's grim confession that for a moment we had forgotten the presence of Angela. By now, she was truly a presence. The mist had grown, seeming to swirl and twist with a life of its own, and now it had formed itself into a discernible resemblance to a woman.

'Johnathon,' I said. 'You've got to take her out the back way, quickly.'

'Not without you,' he said.

'It's all right. Don't worry about me,' I said firmly. 'I'm not afraid of Angela, not now, not ever again. I know her secret. But we must think of Elizabeth. You must take her with you, now.'

'What will you do?' he asked anxiously.

'I only want to talk to Angela,' I told him. 'No, don't look at her. Remember, no one can have any power over our minds unless we allow them to take it.'

'You're sure . . . ?' he asked, hesitating.

'I'm sure. But you must get her out of here, quickly!'

He reached for Elizabeth. She tried to avoid him, but he firmly seized her and lifted her in his arms, ignoring her struggles.

'Don't let her look back,' I said as he started for the rear of the house.

'You have one minute,' he said over his shoulder. 'Then I'm coming back for you if I have to carry you out like this.'

I watched them disappear through the door to Elizabeth's room, and then I turned to face Angela.

When I did, I almost lost my courage. The mist had formed itself into an image of the dead woman. For the first time, I could clearly see her in the same dress she wore in the portrait, her long hair loose and flowing. Even in this supernatural state, her face was beautiful, as beautiful as when that portrait had been painted.

But the difference lay in this: in the portrait, the artist and model had contrived together at that angelic, beatific expression, while what I saw before me was evil itself. Her face, which I could see clearly, was twisted into a grimace of hatred, pure and naked, and her eyes literally glowed with the violence of her emotions. The room seemed to crackle with tension.

The effect was shattering, and I had to fight the urge to turn and flee. But that, I knew, was what she wanted and intended. That was the power that she had over living people, and her only power—their own fear.

'It's no use, Angela,' I said in a soft but even voice. 'I'm not afraid of you now, not any longer.'

I reached for the lamp burning on the console against the wall and lifted it high so that its light shined upon and even through her, diminishing the impact of that horrible leer.

'And that is your only weapon,' I said, taking a step toward her. As I did so, I found my own fear fading, to be replaced by a new confidence. 'Fear, the fear you inspire; that's all you have, all you can do. You can only do to me what you do through me, and that is the truth, is it not?'

She lifted a hand as though she would strike at me. For a reply, I laughed and came closer.

'Go ahead,' I said, holding the lamp before me as if its light were a shield. 'A hand that can pass through a wall cannot strike a blow. Curse me if you like, rail against me. You are helpless, powerless against me because I have the one weapon to defeat you—the truth. I know you, and I know the sham you are.'

I came on slowly but without pause. The mist moved like a living thing, swaying toward me and then abruptly away from me. I was close enough now to reach out and touch her had she been real. I could feel the coldness, numbing in its intensity, and something else, something almost impossible to describe. She was trying to reach me, trying to enter my mind, as she had done before. But then I had been unprepared, and her insidious attack had been unexpected. Now I knew better. I would not succumb to her efforts; still, it was as if her malign impulses were hammering at the closed doors of my mind.

'No,' I said, thrusting the lamp into the mist. 'Not this time. Sham. Fake. That's all you are, all you have ever been, dead or alive.'

Finally, she began to move too, away from me, toward the stairs. She floated like a vapor, up the stairs now, slowly, retreating. And I came after her, still bearing the lamp before me, still lashing her with my scorn.

'No more real when you were alive than you are now,' I continued, my confidence growing. 'All of your artificial piety, all of your fake love. You've never loved, Angela, never. That was all a mask to cover your hatred, your cruelty, your coldness—yes, your coldness—that emanates from you now. It was always there, always the essence of Angela, wasn't it?'

She was backing up the stairs before me now, and the contest of wills had become a storm of fury. You could almost see our opposing impulses grappling together between us. The coldness was unbelievably intense now, and I could feel hatred and evil swirling about me, trying to penetrate the cloak of my scorn. I waved my hand as if to thrust them away.

'Imposter,' I cried, and I could not say whether I was actually shouting now or even speaking aloud. It might have been only my thoughts that I was hurling at that swirling, living mist. 'You are nothing but a joke, Angela, a laugh. We will gather before the fire in the future, and we shall talk about you, and we shall laugh to think that we ever feared you, that we ever cared about your silly and futile haunting.'

We had come to the landing, and here she stopped as if she would make her stand. I was three steps below her, and I too stopped. A wave of hatred, of evil desire, seemed to rush over me, and I faltered. For a moment, almost as if a palpable hand had shoved me, I lost my balance and nearly fell.

But I caught myself and planted my feet squarely, seizing the handrail with my free hand. I threw back my head and hurled my final challenge at her.

'Laugh at you,' I cried. 'As I laugh at you now.'

I laughed. The mist raged, the face vanishing in a cloud. A ghastly greenish glow contested the light from my lamp. The wind rushed about me, howling in my ears until it had become a deafening roar.

'Go back, Angela,' I said, still laughing. 'You can do nothing here. Your power is gone. Go back, back to the hell you came from, back to the hell you created for yourself with all those years of coldness and cruelty. You can do nothing to me that you cannot do through me, and you can never again reach me.'

The forces about me rose to a crescendo. There was no woman before me now, only clouds of mist, all in motion, glowing, chilling.

Suddenly, the lamp in my hand exploded. Fire flung itself everywhere like a living force. It was over me, a searing sheet of flames scorching my dress; it was in the carpet, where a hundred orange tongues flicked to life in an instant; especially, it was in the canvas portrait of Angela. That became in an instant a wall of flame and smoke.

I stumbled, coughing in the smoke and trying to beat out the flames in my skirt. I was surrounded by fire. I tried to run but missed my footing and came down with a crash, striking my head soundly against the wall. For a moment, I was horrifyingly conscious of the fire all about me, enveloping me; then I sank into a semi-consciousness from which I could not rouse myself.

'Angela,' I thought helplessly. 'You've won after all. You've claimed me for your own.'

It seemed to me, dazed as I was, that I heard laughter, the laughter of triumph, but it may only have been my crazed imagination.

Suddenly, I heard another sound, my name being called over and over, it seemed from a great distance.

'Mary!' a voice shouted. I recognized it as Johnathon's.

'Johnathon, I'm here,' I tried to shout, but my lungs burned with the acrid smoke, and nothing came out but a faint squeak.

'Johnathon,' I cried silently, sinking to the floor. 'It is over,' I thought.

*   *   *

But it was not yet over, for suddenly there he was, Johnathon, bending over me, sweeping me up in his arms. I felt his hands on me, beating out the flames; he grabbed a rug from the floor and wrapped me in it, smothering the fire. Then he was carrying me, running down the stairs and out of the house.

The air helped to restore my senses, but for a moment or two, I could do nothing but cough and choke, clinging weakly to his arm and sucking in great mouthfuls of air.

At last, I was able to stand with his help and look at Green Willows.

The house was an inferno. Every window was lighted with the flames that had now eaten their way through the roof and were leaping skyward. Ashes were already drifting down to us on puffs of smoke, and even here in the drive, the heat was growing intense.

For a moment, I stared in both horror and a growing sense of relief; at last, I told myself, the spirits would be laid to rest.

But then, suddenly, I remembered and looked anxiously around. 'Where's Elizabeth?' I asked.

'I put her in the carriage and came back for you,' Johnathon said. He had been staring at the fire too, sadly but resignedly. 'She fainted, so I knew she'd be all right.'

'But she's not here!' I cried, looking into the empty carriage—the light from the fire lit its interior brilliantly, shining into every corner.

'But she must be,' Johnathon said. He looked past me at the emptiness. 'Where could she have gone, unless . . .' He turned and stared again at the fire. 'Oh, my God,' he whispered.

'Johnathon,' I cried, clinging to his arm when he would have raced back to the blazing house. 'You can't. If she's gone in there, it's too late.'

He shook himself free of me. 'I've got to go,' he said and started for the house.

It was futile, though; just then a great section of wall came crashing down. Even Johnathon was driven back by the nightmarish heat. There was nothing left of Green Willows but a tower of flame and, at our backs, the serene beauty of the lake, with the little arched bridge and the white gazebo that Elizabeth had wanted restored.

And Elizabeth, I knew in my heart, was with her mother at last, as she had always wanted.

EPILOGUE

Green Willows is gone.

The grasses have grown tall on the banks of the lake, and the only voices here are the whispering willows. It is dusk, and the shadows are deepening around the gazebo. The stone steps are blurred with moss and approaching night, and the gazebo smells bitter and narcotic, of autumn and stale water. There is much dust and birds' droppings.

'There is no one here,' I tell myself aloud, and the sound of my voice echoes back to me hollowly from the stone walls. The wind murmurs in the willows, and somewhere above, a bird titters.

Angela is gone, and Gina, and little Elizabeth. Gone too is Johnathon, for that bent and emptied man with whom I live is not the strong, sure man I loved.

But I too am only a shadow, a ghost of the girl who once came here.

Ghosts, both of us—all of us—and we belong to Green Willows as surely as Angela or Gina.

And perhaps some day a young couple may stroll this way at dusk. They may sit in the grass by the lake or risk the rotting bridge. They will kiss and whisper together, as young lovers do.

And suddenly, she may look beyond his shoulder and stiffen, and say 'Look,' pointing. And when he asks her what she saw, she will say, 'I thought there were two women there, just on the bank,' or, 'There was a man there, in the shadow of the gazebo, and a young woman running into his arms.'

And he will laugh, tell her she was imagining things, and kiss her again to make her forget.

And we shall go back to Green Willows.

We hope you have enjoyed this Large
Print book. Other Chivers Press or
Thorndike Press Large Print books are
available at your library or directly from the
publishers.

For more information about current and
forthcoming titles, please call or write,
without obligation, to:

Chivers Large Print
published by BBC Audiobooks Ltd
St James House, The Square
Lower Bristol Road
Bath BA2 3BH
UK
email: bbcaudiobooks@bbc.co.uk
www.bbcaudiobooks.co.uk

OR

Thorndike Press
295 Kennedy Memorial Drive
Waterville
Maine 04901
USA
www.gale.com/thorndike
www.gale.com/wheeler

All our Large Print titles are designed for
easy reading, and all our books are made to
last.